TAMED BY THE BERSERKER

THE BERSERKER SAGA
BOOK 12

LEE SAVINO

SILVERWOOD PRESS, LLC

FREE BOOK

TAMED BY THE BERSERKER

"You are wild and disobedient. A threat to yourself and all others. To save your life, we must prove you are bonded and submitted fully to us." His voice was a guttural growl.

I lick my lips and challenged, "And what if you fail?"

Thorsteinn snarled.

"We will not fail," Vik said. "Sorrel, we're going to tame you."

1

S *orrel*

FIRELIGHT PLAYED in the bars of my cage, mottling my bare arms as I chafed them. The wind whispered and whined around the rocky heights, cutting through my jerkin and breeches and tugging at my hair like a band of mischievous demons. My cage swayed in the wind.

Below, far below, down the path and away from the ledge, the warriors built a bonfire higher and higher. Huge logs were sacrificed to feed the fire. Dozens of warriors stood around it, drinking and eating meat and calling out encouragement to build the blaze higher and higher. They'd started the fire at the same time I'd been locked in the cage. A torture of light and heat too far away to feel.

Two warriors emerged from the path and my heart leapt up, only to sink again. These were not my warriors. One waited while the other untied the rope and lowered my cage. With a smirk, he let go when the structure hovered a foot off the ground. The cage crashed down, jarring me. I gritted my teeth and kept my face blank. The guards would not see me cower.

One of them kicked the cage bars with his boot. The warriors busied themselves with the straps to untie the door. Before they came, I'd loosened them myself, only to stop. Escape would've meant I'd had to jump from the height. Even if I hadn't broken bones, I would've had to climb down this part of the rocky mountain, avoiding all the Berserkers who might harm me. According to the shouts drifting up from the bonfire, there were many warriors who did not want to follow the Alpha's order to leave me unharmed until my trial. They wanted my blood.

I was safer in the cage. When the door fell away and the warriors stepped back, I stayed where I was.

One warrior squatted to glower at me.

"Out," he barked. I crawled out of the cage and forced my cramped limbs straight. Even standing, I wasn't half the height of the warriors. They loomed over me, glaring.

"Who gave her breeches?" the first asked.

"It's what she was wearing when we found her," the second tipped his head to the side, studying me.

"She dresses like a man. Unnatural," the first muttered, and turned away.

"Hands," my second jailer ordered, and when I lifted them, he looped a noose around my wrists and pulled it tight, careful not to touch me. They led me from my cage on the ledge down the narrow mountain path towards the bonfire.

A third warrior met us on the path before we stepped into the great clearing. He blocked my path, looming over me. I kept my gaze fixed on his bare chest, refusing to look in his face.

"Ragnar," one of my guards cautioned, but Ragnar waved a hand and they fell silent. Without seeing his face, I felt his rage and disgust, directed at me.

"Rosalind has not woken. The healers say she may never wake." The warrior's voice dropped in pitch, becoming even more guttural. "Her sister mourns."

I closed my eyes and swayed on the path. In my mind's eye, Rosalind lay on the grass, still as death. I didn't need the warrior to tell me what I'd done. What I'd regret for the rest of my life, but did I have a choice?

We stood there for some time, Ragnar blocking my path. The wind tore at my face and hair. Behind me, my guards breathed down my neck. If my guards decided I should die here, now, they could fling me off the ledge. I would be powerless to stop them.

At last Ragnar straightened. "The Alphas are waiting," he said in a clearer voice. "Hurry up."

The guards behind me prodded me forward with their weapons.

As we moved down the path, my knees shook with relief I didn't deserve. I almost wish I'd spoken up, goaded Ragnar until he pushed me to my death. The pain in my heart grew with every step.

We entered the clearing and a thicket of warriors bristling with weapons. They growled as I passed, their hate hitting my face like heat from the roaring inferno. Ahead the bonfire snapped and crackled, its reddish claws tearing into the night sky.

More Berserkers lined my route. The ones in wolf form snarled and snapped at my heels. I set my face in stone, marching past hulking men and giant wolves. They will not see me cry or shrink in fear. Not tonight.

My foot caught a stone, causing me to stumble. A few warriors smirked.

"Careful," one of my guards muttered, but made no move to help me. At last we reached the bonfire and my place to stand judgement. I stepped onto a long flat stone, holding up my chin and keeping my gaze on the fire.

Across the huge bonfire four Alphas ranged on a crop of giant rocks. Two stood with arms crossed over their chests. One sat on a throne-like rock, solemn as a king. The firelight turned his hair to gold. As soon as I was in place, he rose and spread his arms. The assembly fell quiet.

"My brothers, we have gathered to pass judgement on a grave matter. The spaewife Sorrel stands before us accused of treason."

"Murder," someone muttered. Probably Ragnar.

"Silence," the tattooed Alpha growled. "Samuel speaks."

After a pause the seated Alpha, Samuel, continued. "We've heard the story of what happened, as best as we can guess. Three days ago, Sorrel left the safety of our borders and entered the lands controlled by the Corpse King. With her was an unmated spaewife named Rosalind. We do not know why they left. We do not know how they survived three days' journey, even though the Corpse King's soldiers patrolled the area they walked."

"Traitor," a voice at my left spat. "She is in league with the Corpse King." A wolf snarled.

Samuel raised his voice. "We do know how the search patrol found them: Sorrel armed with a sling and pouch of stones, her friend fallen from a blow to the head."

A great murmur flared from the assembled warriors, blending with growls from the wolves.

"Silence," another Alpha ordered the crowd, and the muttering died.

Samuel continued. "We captured both and brought them back here. Sorrel is as you see her. Rosalind lies as if sleeping, suffering from her wound. There is evidence they struggled. If Rosalind dies, Sorrel will be guilty of murder."

I slumped, unable to stand proud any longer. Fatigue rolled over me, a great weight. I bowed my head and closed my eyes.

The warriors shouted around me, calling for my death. "She is guilty. She tried to kill her own friend, one of our treasured spaewives. We found her with the weapon, standing over the unconscious woman."

"Why did she leave the mountain?" One of the Alpha's asked. He didn't raise his voice, but it carried over the roar of the rabble.

"She will not explain why she and Rosalind left the home of unmated spaewives, and escaped the mountain," Samuel said. "She will not speak to answer the Alpha's questions. So, we must draw our own conclusions."

"She did it," someone muttered at my side. Perhaps one of my guards. "She is guilty."

A low growl accompanied the accusation. It cut off suddenly.

"The Corpse King is growing stronger. Every day he batters our defenses. How is it two young women slipped through our fingers, and his?"

"Is it not clear? She was headed for the Corpse King to betray us."

"Treason," one muttered.

"She is in league with the Corpse King," another said, and spat in my direction.

I kept my mouth shut. I still felt the weight of the stone

in my hand, small but deadly. I still heard the whir of the sling as I aimed and saw the bright red blood blossoming from Rosalind's head before she fell. It played over and over in my head, always ending with my friend on the ground, blood leaking from her skull.

My fault.

"Enough," Samuel finally called, and the warriors fell silent.

"Sorrel of the Berserkers, you've been found guilty of betraying the pack, conspiring with the enemy, and harming your own friend. Do you have anything to say?"

I didn't bother to raise my eyes or shake my head. Anything I had to say, I'd already said. The Berserkers who found me standing over Rosalind did not believe my fantastical tale. Why should I repeat it?

The Alpha let the silence stretch one, two more moments before continuing. "Very well. The Alphas will confer to decide your fate. Take her away."

A warrior yanked me from my perch and dragged me past jeering warriors and snarling wolves. We walked up the path a little ways from the standing stones into an alcove in the forest. The great fire reached through the trees to stripe us with its light.

"Here," he pointed to the ground and my heart stopped.

"No please," I whimpered as he dragged me toward a gaping pit. I hadn't begged or pleaded before, but this broke me. "Anywhere but there." I kicked but lost my balance and foothold. The warrior guard would put me in the deep hole and bury me. I'd scream and my mouth would fill with dirt and nothing would save me, nothing—

A roar gusted the leaves around us. The warrior released me and drew his weapon.

"Who's there?"

Something slunk between the trees, shaking the undergrowth.

"Show yourself," my guard whirled to follow, pointing his long knife towards the threat. It roared again, the sound echoing all around and making the guard turn this way and that in panic. Whatever great beast lurked in the gloom, it was hunting, taunting the guard. Now was my chance to run.

I backed to the edge of the clearing, only to slam into a large, hard body.

"Be still," someone growled in my ear. A strong hand coiled loosely about my throat. Shock hit my system, turned my bones to stone.

"Show yourself," the guard cried, unaware that another held me. "Unless you're a coward—" he barely got the word out before a huge silver wolf leapt from the forest and slammed into him.

On instinct, I fought the warrior holding me, thrashing and kicking my feet. He hauled me off the ground, holding me clear by the throat. I flailed harder, my need for escape eclipsed by the need for air.

He dropped me to the ground beside a great pine, and I scrabbled backwards until my back pressed into the bark.

"What—" my words died when I recognized Thorsteinn, saw the rage written on his face.

"Be still," Thorsteinn ordered. He didn't draw a weapon to threaten me. He didn't have to. His human features were transformed into that of a monster. Everything in his hulking body and bright, feral eyes told me he was close to losing control.

I swallowed carefully, my hand at my bruised throat. The monster cocked his head to the side as if waiting for me to panic or run. After a moment he grunted and gave me his back. His giant body blocked me from the raging scuffle between guard and wolf.

When my cruel guard broke away, the wolf let him go, slinking behind Thorsteinn with hackles raised and snarling teeth.

Thorsteinn drew his axe and pointed it toward the sprawled warrior. "Keep your hands off her." His voice was a guttural growl.

The guard rose with hands outstretched. "I meant no disrespect. I did not know she belonged to you."

"Now you do," Thorsteinn hefted his axe and smacked the head against his palm. "You touched what doesn't belong to you. You're lucky I don't take your hands."

The wolf's snarls echoed around the clearing.

"The Alphas ordered—"

"Damn the Alphas," Thorsteinn snapped and roared loud enough to shake the trees. "Go."

The warrior scrambled backwards until he almost fell in the brush before turning and making his escape.

I stood trembling behind Thorsteinn and the wolf. Both glanced back at me, their eyes bonfire bright. There was a sudden wind and the wolf's back arched, his shoulders growing broad as the shaggy form rose from the ground on two legs. The warrior, Vik, stretched into his man form, grimacing and angling his head to crack his neck. When the Change was complete, he wore a silver wolf pelt on his shoulders, and nothing else.

They both turned to me. I shrank against the tree. I'd never been afraid of these warriors, but they were no longer mere men. Their bodies were Changed into something betwixt man-shape and monster. They stood a head taller than me, their eyes bright with the beast, their fingers tipped with massive claws.

"Sorrel," Thorsteinn rasped. He pointed a claw at the ground in front of him. I pushed myself to standing but couldn't make myself move.

"You've returned," I whispered. "You came back for me."

Vik tilted his head, angling his face to sniff the air. "Did you think we would not?"

After they abandoned me? "No."

"Sorrel," Thorsteinn repeated with less patience. "Come here."

Out of habit my back stiffened. "No."

"You will not obey?" Thorsteinn's eyes flashed.

I glared back.

Vik's laugh broke the tense silence. I jumped at the sound and he came at me, his features calm and eyes less bright. "That is the Sorrel I know." He pulled me from my hardened stance, propelling me easily to the center of the clearing. There he proceeded to inspect me from head to boot, running large hands over my head and shoulders, gripping my arms and coasting over my hips and legs. He raised my bound hands but didn't free me.

"Unharmed?" Thorsteinn growled.

Vik grunted.

You could've just asked me. I glared at Thorsteinn, but he didn't respond. He stood tense beside us, his clawed hands fisted as if holding tight to the last of his control.

Vik examined my fingers, testing each one as making sure they still had feeling. He checked my skull for bumps and even my ears.

Satisfied I was whole, he stepped away and nodded to Thorsteinn.

I licked my lips. "Happy now?"

Now Thorsteinn did meet my eyes. "No." In a flash, he closed in. Clamping a hand around my neck, he backed me into a tree trunk. I stared at him, my feet scrabbling on the ground, unable to find a foothold. He held me aloft with an iron arm, his palm covered my windpipe, firm but not crushing. My breath came in spurts as he touched his brow to mine and growled in a voice more wolf than human, "Why did you leave the mountain?"

"I had to—"

He snarled. "Did we mean so little to you, that you would run?"

Run from them? They left me first. "You were gone," I sneered. "I did not think of you at all." That was not true, and he would know it. But I would deny otherwise to the last.

"Lies." Thorsteinn's hold tightened. His eyes were a blinding yellow, fur starting to ripple down his arm. He was close to a Change.

"Thorsteinn," Vik called a warning, and the enraged warrior let me down. My legs crumpled and I would've fallen if he didn't support me.

"Steady," he murmured, his voice clearer. I gulped and dropped my gaze. The beast was close.

I couldn't stop myself from baiting it. "Why do you care?"

Thorsteinn snarled and started for me again, and Vik stopped him with a hand. "Choking her will not show her you care," he said in his usual half mocking, half amused tone. Vik waited for Thorsteinn's agreeing grunt to turn to me. "Do not toy with us, Sorrel. You know very well we care."

"I know you left me at the home of the unmated spaewives." I crossed my arms and stared at the ground. "I don't know why you returned."

Vik and Thorsteinn exchanged glances. "We were on

patrol near the Corpse King's lair when the word came of what you had done.," Vik said. "We ran day and night to reach you before the trial."

"We could not believe," Thorsteinn started in a choked, guttural voice, then stopped. After a few heaving breaths he continued in a more normal voice. "We could not believe the reports we were hearing. Two spaewives left the lodge where they were protected by countless guards and magic and ventured beyond the borders of the mountain. Slipped past the guard and patrols and ran straight into enemy territory."

"Seems we trained you too well to move with stealth," Vik murmured.

"What possessed you to run?" Thorsteinn asked in a growl.

Biting my lip, I stared at the ground. He shook me by the scruff of my neck, as a dog shakes a misbehaving puppy.

"Sorrel?" Vik squatted close. "Answer us."

"No," I whispered, barely a sound escaping between my lips.

"You will tell us," Thorsteinn growled with another shake. "We will make you tell us."

They could. They could make me. After blurting the story to the uncaring Berserkers who found me standing over Rosalind, it would be a relief to be heard. Not the whole story—I couldn't risk it. Couldn't do that to Rosalind. I may have killed her, I couldn't slander her name. Tell all she betrayed the pack. Even if it was true.

"I left because Rosalind did," I blurted and paused to see how they'd react.

"Rosalind left first?" Vik cocked his head. Both warriors' faces were blank.

"She did. She left in the middle of the night and I followed."

"She left," Vik repeated. He and Thorsteinn exchanged glances. I could see the doubt in their eyes.

Rage flashed through me. "Why should I tell you anything," I hissed, "if you're not going to believe any of it?"

"Rosalind was in the lodge with her sister Aspen. Reports say she and Aspen were close. Why did she leave her sister on a fool's errand?"

"I don't know." I wilted a little. "I didn't ask her." I had been too busy trying to keep us alive.

"Whereas you spoke openly of leaving, of heading into the wilderness to make a living as a hunter. That was your plan even when you were back at the abbey." Thorsteinn prodded me. "Is it not so?"

"It's true," I whispered. Everything about me spoke against what actually happened. No wonder everyone thought I was lying.

I had hoped Thorsteinn and Vik would at least try to believe me. But perhaps it was easier if they did not. I could protect Rosalind and keep the secret of what she'd done.

"You followed her off the mountain for three days. Why did you finally strike her?" Thorsteinn shook me when I remained silent. "Answer me!"

"Thorsteinn," Vik cautioned, and the enraged warrior released me. I slumped forward, right into Vik's arms.

"Sorrel—" he started.

A twig snapped at the entrance to the clearing and Thorsteinn whirled with a roar.

Ragnar appeared between the tall pines, his hands upraised to prove he brought no weapons. "The Alphas will see you now. They're ready to pass sentence."

Thorsteinn snarled. Vik rose, a steadying hand on my back. "We're coming. Tell the Alphas we will bring her."

Ragnar nodded and melted into the shadows.

Thorsteinn dropped to his knees before me. He drew up my chin with one claw-tipped finger.

"You will say nothing, do nothing. Look at no one. Do you understand?" When I only stared at him, his features rippled with the power of the Change. "You will submit to us. Say it. Promise you will submit."

"Sorrel," Vik said more patiently. "This is a matter of life or death. The pack is calling for your blood. You must do as we say, nothing more, nothing less. If you do not," he shot an amused look at his seething warrior brother. "Thorsteinn will Change into a beast and challenge all of the Alphas. All will be lost."

"Promise," Thorsteinn barked.

I looked from warrior to warrior. Faces so familiar but now so distant.

"I promise."

A small smile touched Vik's lips. "Good girl." His eyes flashed with his usual humor.

Thorsteinn still regarded me like the enemy. With a grunt, he rose to his feet and strode ahead. Vik planted himself behind me, propelling me forward with his hands on my shoulders. I went willingly until we reached the edge of the fire and angry warriors.

"Look at no one but Thorsteinn or me," Vik reminded me. I fixed my eyes on Thorsteinn's boots. It had been a long time since I had to pretend to be docile. I was never any good at it.

"Murderer," a warrior hissed, and I flinched. Vik snarled at him.

When we reached the Alphas, I started to walk towards

the sentencing stone, but Vik stopped me with his hands securely on my shoulders. Thorsteinn stood before and Vik behind, blocking me from the pack's gaze.

"Thorsteinn, Vik," the head Alpha greeted them. "You've returned."

"Just in time," the tattooed Alpha muttered.

"Where have you been?" another Alpha asked.

"We traveled far on patrol, almost to the cave of the Corpse King. We spent days eluding the clutches of the enemy while spying," Vik answered.

"Why would you accept such a dangerous patrol and leave behind the one you claimed?" Samuel's eyes were bright.

Thorsteinn shrugged. "We are experienced scouts, too valuable to keep home. That is why we both went."

"And the accused spaewife is your mate?"

Vik's hands squeezed on my shoulders. I did not understand his reassurance until Thorsteinn said, "No."

A loud murmur went up from the waiting crowd. Warriors muttering, protesting, calling for my blood.

"Silence," one of the Alphas roared again and again. "Silence!"

I stood frozen under the weight of Vik's hands. Thorsteinn stared ahead, his face stern and unyielding as the rock of the mountain. I wished he would look at me.

Vik squeezed my tight shoulders again.

"Explain," the Alpha called Samuel ordered. "You claimed this spaewife in front of the pack and promised to keep her from all harm. Why do you say she is not your mate?

"Because it's true. We claimed her and hoped the bond would form. But it did not. And so, we left her at the lodge of unmated spaewives and went on patrol. It was clear she had not bonded. And now we know for sure. Sorrel was plotting all along to escape us. She pretended to be close to us so we would trust her. But as soon as she could, she ran. We believe she convinced Rosalind to go along with her, but they quarreled at the last. Perhaps Rosalind wanted to return, and Sorrel disagreed. The fight escalated and grew violent. Maybe they knew the Berserkers were tracking them, and Sorrel grew desperate and struck Rosalind down."

Thorstein's story hit me like a blow. They didn't listen to a single word I said. They didn't believe me. I swayed and would've fallen if Vik hadn't tightened his hold on me. The warriors around me rumbled and beat their shields, crying for my punishment and death. Thorsteinn never looked my way.

Why are you saying this? I wanted to scream. Of all the Berserkers, I would've thought Thorsteinn and Vik would not think the worst of me. *If they would not believe me, who would?*

"We knew something was wrong, but we did not suspect this level of planning," Vik added.

"Sorrel never bonded with us. We did all we could, but she never was truly ours. That is why we sent her to the home of unmated spaewives before we left for patrol." Thorsteinn turned his head, and in an awful finality met my gaze. "Sorrel was never our mate."

I DON'T KNOW what happened after that. The warriors shouted, the Alpha's couldn't keep order. The smoke rose up and choked me until I coughed, unsteady on my feet. My eyes stung and the world turned grey. I could no longer see the tall form of Thorsteinn, his broad arms crossed over his tattooed chest. Or Vik, rubbing his beard, no sign of his usual good humor.

Never our mate. Never our mate. The echo rose up with the hellish flames, drowning everything else out, stabbing me in the chest. I gasped against the pain.

"Take her away. Hold her until sentencing," one of the Alphas ordered. Someone grasped the rope tying my arms and pulled me off the stone. The angry voices faded as I was tugged out of the clearing. I staggered and a hand came to my side.

"Easy," a deep voice murmured. Vik. I jerked backwards, away from him. My body and soul were alive with pain, shredded by what they'd said. All the time in our home together. All the sweet moments I'd had with them. All the trust I'd given, pieces of my heart I'd sacrificed. In the span of one short speech, everything we'd given each other was destroyed.

You told them we weren't mated, I wanted to scream. *Why would you lie?*

"Sorrel," Vik started, but Thorsteinn raised a hand to silence him. "Not here." Thorsteinn tugged on the rope binding my hands. "Come," he said to me, but I planted my feet, glaring at him.

"Sorrel," Thorsteinn's tone when he said my name was nothing like Vik's. The grey-eyed warrior matched my glare, his lips pressed together and heavy brows slanting down. "You will obey," he growled.

No. I didn't have to speak aloud for him to hear my answer. Power poured into Thorsteinn's gimlet glare and calcified, turning his eyes gold. Beside us, Vik sighed and crossed his arms over his chest.

There was a long pause. My stomach flip flopped but I held my ground. They knew how stubborn I was. It probably wasn't wise to bait these warriors, but when had that ever stopped me?

Thorsteinn straightened. "Very well," he ground out, his eyes glowing with uncanny light. "We do this the hard way."

I stepped back as he crowded me, but didn't get far before I was up, up, tossed over his shoulder with my stomach in my throat and hair in my face. Thorsteinn clapped a hand on my bottom and tightened his grip on my legs. I couldn't kick and punching his back would do as much good as a pebble bouncing off a mountain face. I fisted my hands in his jerkin, hanging on as he strode down the path.

When I raised my head, Vik had a hand over his mouth as if smoothing his beard. His eyes crinkled as if he hid a smile. When he dropped his hand, his face was solemn, but he winked at me.

Thorsteinn picked up his pace. The dark settled over us as the warriors left the path and plunged into the forest, weaving through the trees.

I was tired and dizzy by the time Thorsteinn set me down at the base of the massive tree that held our home. *Their home,* I corrected myself. If I wasn't their mate, I was no longer welcome.

I huddled on the ground as Vik climbed the footholds and tossed down the rope. Thorsteinn attached the rope to the basket I hadn't seen since I first laid eyes on the tree.

～

THEN

"WHAT IS THIS PLACE?" I asked.

Vik grinned, flashing white teeth. "We call it 'Yggdrasil'. The tree that holds the worlds."

I squinted up at the giant ash. The canopy spread larger than the roof of any building I'd seen.

"He jests," Thorsteinn shook his head. I was used to their rhythm. Vik joked, and Thorsteinn pretended to disapprove, keeping his smiles to himself. "The real 'Yggdrasil' is the tree of life, or the world tree. It holds the nine worlds, including Asgard, home of the gods."

"There's only one God," I corrected automatically, and covered my mouth, horrified to hear the teachings of the nuns spilling out of my mouth.

"Really?" Vik cocked his head. "Is that what you believe?"

I gulped, but both Vik and Thorsteinn watched me closely, as if truly interested in what I had to say. It was stupid to argue with these warriors after all we'd been through, but I'd never been good at holding in my thoughts. I had the scars on my back to prove it.

"I don't know what I believe."

The warriors shrugged and went back to what they were doing, rigging some sort of rope system over one of the high branches. They'd nailed boards to the trunk, too. Thorsteinn climbed up and attached the rope to a basket hidden by the leaves.

The wind came and the tree tossed its green head, the canopy rustling like a thousand birds. High above us, nestled between the thickest branches, freshly hewn boards made a platform. When I backed up, the rest of the structure came into sight—a house, built from wood and thatch and lashed to the living tree.

When I thought of it, sawdust had littered the path leading to the ash.

"Did you build that?" I pointed.

Vik nodded. "Do you like it?" He took a handful of my hair and tugged playfully. "We thought you would, little squirrel."

I swatted at him and he laughed. I shouldn't be so comfortable with my captors, but Vik was easy to talk to, easy to like.

"I'm not a squirrel," I mumbled.

"And yet you always seem to be climbing trees," he said, amused.

Thorsteinn jumped down, holding the basket. It's wide and deep, big enough to fit a small body. Like mine.

"Please," I backed up, stopping when I run into Vik's legs and looking up. "Do I have to ride in the basket? Can you teach me to climb instead?"

"You wish to climb?" Thorsteinn asked. Of the two warriors, he most intimidated me, but now his voice was gentle. He squatted before me, so tall our heads were almost level. For once, he's looking up to me with his serious grey eyes.

I nodded.

"All right, little warrior. You may climb, if you go slowly and follow instruction. And—" he held out his hand and Vik passed him a free rope. "You must wear a harness. We've come too far and gone through too much to risk you falling now."

I nodded again, resisting the urge to squirm or rub my leg. It was healed, the skin unscarred and unbroken, but I remembered the crack of bone, the blinding pain and bright blood slipping down my thigh.

Vik cleared his throat and I realized I had raised my hand to my shoulder, unconsciously rubbing the marked skin.

Thorsteinn's brow furrowed as he lifted my makeshift jerkin to check the spot I rubbed. "Does it still hurt?"

The bite marks on my neck throbbed at the question, sensitive but not painful. Thorsteinn studied the mark, the skin smooth and healed, a red shiny weal the only evidence of the two warrior's savagery. "No."

Thorsteinn and Vik exchanged glances. There was a long pause while they seemed to communicate silently.

Finally, Thorsteinn rose.

"We'll teach you to climb. First the rope." He wrapped the long rope around me, looping it around my waist and over my shoulders and around my legs. I held still, breathless at his touch. When he was done his eyes were bright gold. He was affected too.

Vik joined us, running his hands over my body and testing the harness.

"You will follow our lead and do as we say," Thorsteinn lectured me. He often gave the orders while Vik made the jokes.

Sure enough, as Thorsteinn frowned at his knots, Vik caught my eye and winked at me.

I hid a giggle as Thorsteinn straightened.

"Promise me, Sorrel."

"I'll be good. I promise."

"Good girl." The nerves in my belly lessened at his soft praise.

We faced the tree. Vik climbed the first rungs, pointing out the footholds as I watched. The bearded warrior was all seriousness.

Thorsteinn's hands rested around my waist, holding me back until Vik finished his instruction.

"Ready?" his breath stirred my hair.

I swallowed. I've travelled with these warriors for days now. We've hiked and hidden from our enemies, ran and made camp in dark shelters. We'd gone through many perils and almost didn't survive. They captured me and took me from my home but kept me safe.

Now we were safe in Berserker territory, and they showed no sign of letting me go. And a part of me didn't want them too. With them, I had more freedom than I'd ever known. They were my captors, but treated me like an equal, a sister, a friend.

I didn't understand how I felt about them.

"I'm ready." I placed my hands on the holds above my head and waited for Thorsteinn to boost me up.

"Go slowly. Wait for Vik," he went on ordering me.

"I will." The less I argued, the more I obeyed, the more independence they allowed.

"Good girl." He lifted me into place, and I clung to the tree trunk, pressing to the bark and gripping the holds like a squirrel.

"Sorrel," Thorsteinn called and I twisted to meet his rare smile. For once he'd lost his stern look and his happy look did things to my insides I didn't want to think about. "Welcome to your new home."

∼

Now

I SHOOK my head at Thorsteinn as he drew near with the basket. "I want to climb up as I did before."

Thorsteinn studied me. "Do you promise to obey my commands? Do as we say from now on?"

In answer, I just glared at him. I should promise and be done with it, but if they renounced me, what life did we have together?

"Very well," Thorsteinn growled, and tossed me in. I thrashed but as soon as I found my feet, I was already aloft.

So, I was not to be trusted with a climb I'd made many times before. I glared at the enclosure of woven rushes, wondering what they'd do if I wrenched myself up and threw myself to the ground. Probably leave me there for the night, broken bones and all.

So much had changed...

"Here we are," Vik leaned over me, guiding the basket onto a sturdy wooden ledge. He'd climbed ahead as Thorsteinn had pulled me aloft. I peered over the side of the basket to the warrior far below, gripping the rope. Once the basket was secure high in the tree, Vik helped me out. "First things first." His knife flashed and my bonds fell away.

I rubbed my sore wrists as Vik tossed the rope aside.

"Let me see," He raised my wrist, grimacing at the chafed skin. "These should be healing." The mating bond allowed me to share the Berserker healing power.

I stared at the raw wounds. First, they denied our bond, then they expected it to heal me.

As if understanding my thoughts, Vik tucked a strand of hair behind my ear. "The bond worked, once."

The spot between my shoulder and neck twinged, and I covered it with my hand.

"What bond?" I snapped. "You heard Thorsteinn. There is none."

Vik frowned. "Thorsteinn said that for a reason."

"What reason?"

"We'll tell you," Thorsteinn's voice boomed through the tree lodge. He pulled himself onto the platform and drew up the rope ladder behind him. "But first you must answer our questions."

He stalked towards me and my heart pounded faster. I wasn't afraid of him—I'd never been afraid—but my body couldn't help recoiling from him, falling into old roles. He the predator, me the prey.

"Why did you run, Sorrel?"

I pressed my lips together. Thorsteinn's eyes sparked.

"Why would you leave the mountain? What reason could you possibly have?"

I looked to Vik for defense, but the bearded warrior stood back, face inscrutable, arms crossed over his chest as his warrior brother plowed on.

"Do you have any idea how it felt to learn you had run away?" In the darkness of what used to be our dwelling, I couldn't make out Thorsteinn's expression, but there was no mistaking the rage in his tone. "To know you were off the mountain, away from the boundaries that kept you safe. After all we had given you. After all we had done. Do you know how it feels," he advanced on me, the floorboards shaking as he stomped to loom over me, "to know the woman you fought for, cared for, coddled and claimed had rejected your protection and run into the arms of the enemy?"

I should cower. I should be frightened. But I have never been frightened of these warriors—not from the first. And I would not start now.

"You left me," I shouted, leaping to my feet. I stood a full head shorter, but I drew myself up to the last inch, clenched my fists and bawled into his face. "You returned me to the home of unmated spaewives."

"We had a mission," Thorsteinn snapped. "We sent you to where we knew you'd be safe. And then we get word that you had left the lodge. Left the mountain entirely! Snuck past patrols and run unchecked into the enemy's territory." Thorsteinn ran a hand through his hair, gripping the base of his braid in a gesture I knew well. He tugged his braid often when he was frustrated with me. "How far were you going to run, Sorrel? How long before the enemy found and killed you?" His roar shook the walls. My hair flew back but I stood firm against the blast. "You could've died out there." He raged, pacing back and forth. Behind him, Vik stroked his beard.

I scoffed. As if they were worried about me. "Don't pretend you care about me. Not after you left me."

"We care," Vik put in. "We ran from our post scouting the enemy's lair, all the way back here. Only to find you on trial and the pack calling for your blood."

A lump formed in my throat. I knew they cared for me, but they'd taken a patrol deep in Corpse King's territory. I begged to go with them, but they left me at the lodge with the unmated spaewives. At first, I thought they'd come back, but moons passed, and I finally realized they no longer wished to keep me as mate. Or so I thought—

"Months we spent at your side. Taking our time, teaching you to trust. And then you repay us by running. Tell me, Sorrel," Thorsteinn fisted his hand in my short hair, drawing my head back. "Did you think you were fooling us? Biding your time, earning our trust... were you waiting all this time to run?"

Heat suffused my body, followed by chill. They didn't believe me. No one did. But of all those who thought the worst of me, Thorsteinn and Vik's distrust felt the worst. A betrayal.

I would never trust anyone again.

"Was it all to fool us?" Thorsteinn tightened his grip on my hair until the sting brought tears to my eyes. But I would never let them fall. "Answer me."

"Let go of me," I growled at him. The Berserkers aren't the only ones who can growl. "You have nothing to say to me. You rejected me before the pack." *Made up awful stories. Portrayed me in the worst light.*

"To save your life, lass," Vik spoke up. "Part of our plan."

"What do you mean?"

Thorsteinn raised a hand, cutting off Vik's answers. "You do not get to ask questions. Not until you explain to us the real reason why you ran."

"I told you, I followed Rosalind," I said, knowing they would not believe me.

"How did you make it off the mountain?"

"I used the training you gave me. I tracked Rosalind. There were a few warriors on patrol, but it was easy to slip past them."

"How did Rosalind get past them if she was not with you?"

"I don't know." I had a guess, but to speak of it would name Rosalind traitor. And I was not a traitor. Even when the nuns beat me, I had never told on my friends.

"Sorrel—" Thorsteinn growled.

"What's it to you?" I blurted. "You already decided what happened. You told the Alphas I was plotting all along. You think I did this."

"We had to tell them that—" Vik began, but Thorsteinn chopped his hand to silence him.

"We said what we had to say to save you," Thorsteinn rasped.

"You should've let me be." I glared at the floor.

"You'd rather we threw you to the mercy of the pack? There was no mercy for you. We were your only hope."

I snorted even as my heart sank. It was true. The pack hated me. If the spaewives, my friends from the orphanage, heard what I had done to Rosalind, they would hate me. These warriors were all I had left.

And they'd thrown me to the wolves.

Vik and Thorsteinn left me crouched on the floor boards as they made a fire in a great carved stone they hoisted into the tree for this purpose. When smoke spiraled up from the small blaze, Thorsteinn squatted close.

"Because of the story we told the Alphas, they handed you into our care. We can protect you now."

"You lied to them," I whispered. "You said horrible things."

"To save you," he insisted. "You would not speak, so we had to say something." His voice gentled. "If you tell us the truth, we will work to make things right."

I stared into his glowing eyes.

Never our mate. I thought I owed them my life and safety. But after all I had given them, my heart and my trust, they had rejected me. I would never give an inch or a quarter. I would never give them anything willingly again.

Thorsteinn

Thorsteinn, stop, Vik said directly into my head. *She's not listening. The more you shout, the more stubborn she gets.*

I straightened. He was right. Sorrel stared at a point past my head, her brows knotted, and mouth pressed shut. The picture of a woman preparing for a brutal, endless battle.

For a moment, another face flashed in my memory. I remained frozen as Vik stepped around me.

"If you will not speak, you will eat," he ordered. When Sorrel made no move to obey, he gripped her arm and drew her to the fireside.

I stood, frowning at everything and nothing as Vik coaxed Sorrel to accept some bread and dried meat. She barely took anything and after washing her face and hands, he sent her to bed.

She fell asleep before he covered her with a pelt, her brow still creased even as her mouth went slack with exhaustion.

Are you going to stand there all night? Vik asked.

She's not Hildr.

I know, I returned. I pushed thoughts of Hildr away, but not in time for Vik to not see in my memories.

Sorrel will not share Hildr's fate, Vik said.

"Not if I can help it," I spoke aloud. At my feet, Sorrel twitched in her sleep. *I will not let them kill her.*

They will not. We will see to it. Vik joined me in gazing down at our sleeping woman. *We will claim her. We will teach her to be ours.*

I will go to the Alphas and plead her case. Watch over her, I said to Vik. *Tell me when she wakes. We will not leave her alone, not once.*

Never again, Vik agreed. He moved to sit close to her, and I stopped him with a hand on his arm.

No matter what the Alphas say, we must do what needs to be done.

Vik clasped my hand. *We will. I'm with you brother.*

We waited too long to make her ours, I continued. *Now we must make her understand. It will be hard, because she does not trust us. But there is a way. Pleasure her when she obeys, punish her when she rebels.*

Vik grinned. *She is strong. She can take it.*

I thumped his shoulder and left the lodge. Vik was still grinning, probably imagining all the punishments we could use to chastise our mate. To him this was a game, but I knew better. This was life or death. From now on, I make the rules. She will follow them or face the consequences. I will never let anyone in my care be hurt again.

~

SORREL

UNDER YGGDRASIL'S GIANT CANOPY, I slipped in and out of dreams that were not dreams, but memories. I remembered the first moment I first saw Vik and Thorsteinn...

~

THEN

"*STAY BACK,*" *I forced the words out. My fingers gripped my small bow and arrow. If the nuns found me with such a weapon, they'd beat me half dead. So, I hid them with the rest of my belongings in the stillroom, where the nuns were not allowed.*

The abbey was under attack. Underneath the stillroom table, Fern and one of the young orphan girls cowered. A warrior hunted me, a demon-eyed invader with an axe and long knife in his belt and a grey pelt over his shoulders. He held up his hands, weapon free.

"No need to fear, little warrior," he crooned. But at his feet, a giant creature prowled—an enormous white and grey wolf with glowing eyes. The warrior murmured something else and the wolf stepped forward.

I jerked my bow towards the creature. "I'll shoot you."

The warrior chuckled.

And the impossible happened. The wolf hunched and

changed, its back lengthening and body reshaping. My hair blew back from my face, though there should be no wind in this small, underground room. A flash and a man stood before me, a second hard-muscled warrior naked but for a grey and white fur pelt across his shoulders.

The colors of the pelt matched the fur of the disappeared wolf. It could not be. It was not possible.

The warrior who was once a wolf reached out and plucked my weapons from my nerveless grasp. I flinched but he had me out and wrapped in his arms, my back to his chest. I kicked and struggled but he held me fast.

"Got her," his voice rumbled, more like a wolf's growl than the speech of a man. "She's a fighter."

My mind separated from my body and I thrashed as hard as I could. I pushed and contorted against my captor's iron hold, but his grip did not budge. He carried me past the first warrior towards the steps to the abbey.

"Easy," the first soothed, and held up my bow and arrows, an amused look on his face. "Hush, little warrior, I'll bring your weapons. We'll let you use them again, once we get you to safety."

I called to mind all the worst curses I'd ever heard and used them all. The warrior holding me laughed, climbing the stairs, stepping aside to make way for two more warriors. My captor clamped me tighter, squeezing the air from my lungs. I cursed, struggling to move, to breathe.

The first warrior I'd met emerged from the stillroom.

"It's all right, little warrior. You're safe with us." And with that, he ran to the end of the hall and leapt through the broken window. My captor followed, landing on his feet with the soft grace of a cat. Without hesitation, the two men raced to the forest, plunging into the dark.

I don't know how long they carried me or the direction they went. Branches slapped at my body, but the warrior holding me shielded me. He ran uphill and down, around lichen covered boulders and over small streams. My arms froze. I wish I had thought to pull on makeshift trousers and boots under my nightgown. I'd hidden them in the stillroom, where the nuns would never find them. In the confusion of the attack on the abbey, I'd grabbed my bow and arrow, but not thought to change into warrior garb. I'd been too busy fighting, trying to protect Fern and one of the young ones.

As my captor paused on a moonlight hill, I spared a thought for my captive sisters. Where were the warriors taking us? Would we be enslaved or killed?

"Here," I'd given up on hope when the warrior dropped me to my feet. I would've crumpled to the forest floor, but he steadied me until I could stand on my own. I pushed him and backed away.

"Careful. You'll muddy the water." Again, that amused tone.

My feet splashed into a flow of water, a brook welling up over the carpet of dead leaves. I froze, wondering if I could run.

The first warrior appeared before me. "We'll make camp here. Drink while we make a fire. Try to escape and we'll bind your hands."

I stared up at him. The moonlight softened the sharp lines of his face

I shivered.

The warrior shifted his stance over me. He raised his hands and I flinched, but he only smoothed back my hair.

He dropped the pelt over my shoulders. I huddled under the heavy pelt, letting the warmth of his body seep into my chilled skin.

I crouched and drank.

He turned to speak to his fellow warrior, and I threw myself into the bushes beside him, fighting through them to escape into the night.

I KICKED my legs in the air as the long-haired warrior carried me back the way I'd come.

He'd caught me easily, letting me weave through the trees and brush. When I finally realized he was tiring me out, and dropped to my belly under a thorny bush, he reached down and plucked me from my hiding place before I knew what was happening.

These warriors moved with greater stealth and skill than I'd ever seen. They were stronger, so much stronger than me. I was a fool if I thought I could fight them. But I'd rather die a fool than submit.

Firelight winked through the trees, a dark shape moving between us and the small flames. The bearded warrior had built it while the other had fetched me from my failed escape. I dug my fingers in the leather jerkin, tears pricking my eyes at how help-less I was.

My captor crouched next to the fire and rolled me off his shoulder, catching my ankles and binding them together before I could think to kick.

"There," he left me lying on my side, facing the small blaze. I lay stunned a moment, my cheek buried in soft fur. He'd placed me on a wolf pelt.

"We have a warrior in the making," he announced to his comrade.

"I see that," the other replied from his seat on a rock next to the fire. He grinned at me, showing white fangs, and stroked his beard. "She is fierce."

The warrior who'd tied me returned, brushing back my hair. I jerked away from his touch, propping myself up. He wasn't intim-idated by my glare. Instead, he studied me, cocking his head to the side. "What's your name, little fighter?"

I pressed my lips together and refused to answer. With a sigh, my questioner rose and stalked away.

The grinning one took his place. "Come on," he reached out to tug a lock of my hair. My arm whipped out and batted him away before I froze like a rabbit cornered by a large wolf. I couldn't fight these warriors. They could snap my neck without even trying. I cringed, waiting for a blow to fall.

But the bearded warrior did not retaliate. Throwing back his head, he laughed.

"Wait until she bites you," the first said.

"I think not." The warrior in front of me caught my hands before I knew what he was doing and bound them tight.

"There." He sat back on his haunches. I glared at him. I could scoot and try to kick him, but how much good would that do? Trepidation rippled in my belly, threatening to take over.

The long-haired warrior called across the fire, "We'd rather not bind you. But if you insist on fighting..." he shrugged.

"No need to fight us. We're on your side," the warrior close to me winked.

I shook my head at him. What did he mean? This made no sense.

"That's Thorsteinn." he spoke the unfamiliar name in an accent I'd never heard before. "I'm Vik. We'll know your name when you're ready to tell us. Until then, we'll call you 'shield maiden'."

I stared at him. Was he making fun of me? Somehow that was worse than them hurting me.

He dug in his pouch and held a piece of dried meat to my mouth.

"Here. Eat."

I hesitated and he shook it. "Take it. You must eat to keep your strength if you are to fight us."

Darting my head forward, I snapped the food out of his hand.

He chuckled and fished in his pouch for another, holding it to my mouth after I had swallowed. I chewed the second piece more slowly, my eyes darting around the clearing. The warrior didn't bother to hide his scrutiny of me. His large hand circled one ankle. I tried to pull away and he clucked. "You're bleeding. We must care for you better."

The other warrior, Thorsteinn, stalked over. He tore a piece of his jerkin off, and, wetting it in the stream, used it to clean the cuts on my legs as Vik held me still. By the end, I stopped fighting. Vik offered me more meat, a reward for submitting to their ministrations.

When Thorsteinn was done, he gripped my knee and fixed me with his grey-eyed gaze. "No more running. We'll protect you."

I scoffed and looked away, only to catch Vik's eye.

He winked again. "In time you will believe us."

I DID NOT BELIEVE THEM. How could I? They'd stolen me from my home. A home I hated, but the only home I'd known.

I continued to make plans to escape. I tore the bottom half of my nightrobe into strips and used rope to bind them around my legs. The warriors studied me but said nothing about my makeshift breeches.

The next time I woke, a pair of boots and a set of clothes had been placed by my head. Not a dress—a jerkin and pair of long breeches. At first, I couldn't believe it. Had fairies come in the night and gifted me with what I most wanted?

I quickly pulled the breeches on under my robe, crouching to dress so as not to show any skin. When I was done, I didn't recognize myself.

"Shield maiden," Vik said.

Thorsteinn stalked across the campsite. He looked me up and

down but didn't touch me. At last he handed me my bow and
arrows. "As promised," he told me gravely. I blinked. He'd said
he'd return them, but after I had tried to shoot him in the abbey, I
didn't think he would actually let me be armed. "Use them to
defend yourself."

"Against you?" I'd been brave enough to ask. Vik guffawed.
Thorsteinn looked at me a moment, then grasped the back of my
neck and pulled my forehead to his.

"Shoot us and we'll never arm you again."

I nodded. What choice did I have?

But standing in warrior's garb, armed like an equal, it was
easy to agree.

IN TIME, the warriors explained why they had come to the abbey.

"There is a mage who feeds on the magic of spaewives,"
Thorsteinn said. "He was coming for you and the other spaewives
in the abbey."

My face must've shown confusion, for Vik laughed and
explained, "A spaewife is a woman with magic." He tugged a lock
of my hair, chuckling when I pushed his hand away.

"Like a witch?" I asked. The friar had spoken against witches.

"Different magic," Vik said.

Thorsteinn continued, "The mage married many women and
grew in power until one of his wives rose up and bound him for a
thousand years. The spell wore off, and now he has returned."

"We call him the Corpse King," Vik said. Both warriors looked
grim, their hands going to their weapons as if checking to make
sure they were still armed. "He has the power to raise the dead
and make them his slaves."

"Draugr. That is the word for his undead servants,"
Thorsteinn added.

I shivered but thought Vik and Thorsteinn were exaggerating. Doing what men do and making the enemy sound like the most powerful force anyone had ever faced. Even if it was true, I had faith in these warriors. I shouldn't trust the men who stole me from my home, but something about them made me feel safe. They could face anything, even an undead army—not that they were real. It wasn't true, I told myself. It was just a story.

The next day, we ran into a party of draugr. A fetid mist rolled over the hills, choking us as it robbed our sight.

"Run," Thorsteinn ordered, and I did. We raced through patches of the stinking fog. For a moment it cleared, and we scaled a hill, dropping to our bellies to peek over the rise.

"There," Vik pointed at a grey river of moving bodies, laden with spears and shields. At a distance, the draugr looked like men. When they came closer, I caught glimpses of their decaying faces and rotting skin.

With a gasp, I threw myself on my back behind the rise.

"They cannot see us," Thorsteinn gripped my arm to steady me. "But the contingent can sense us. Your magic calls them."

I frowned at my chest. I'd never thought of myself as having magic. I had many sins, but being a witch wasn't one of them.

"Look," Vik nodded to the mist creeping up the hill behind us. "There are two forces."

Thorsteinn swore.

Goosebumps broke over my skin. My stomach flipped, turning to stone. "We're trapped."

"Not yet," Thorsteinn pulled me up and propelled me forward. Slowly, we crept along the rise.

"You do as I say, when I order it and not a moment sooner," the big warrior whispered in my ear. I nodded.

We slunk between the enemy's lines, hiding behind rock croppings and weaving through trees. When the mist grew thick,

Thorsteinn guided me with slight touches, his breath on the back of my neck as I inched along the ridge.

At last the mist cleared. The thumping of marching draugr faded in the distance. We had outpaced them. I had snuck around the abbey plenty, but never with such high stakes or with such able comrades. Despite the danger, my nerves hummed with triumph.

I made a mistake. I looked back. A massive beast with glowing eyes loomed over me, fur sprouting from its giant body. Its face was a long muzzle, black-furred like a wolf's, but it stood on two legs like a man. One hand held an axe. The other was tipped in viscous claws.

I opened my mouth, but nothing came out. Every instinct screamed at me to 'run!'

"Stay calm—" the monster had Thorsteinn's voice.

I flung myself off the path. The hill was steep, and the fall claimed me. I flailed as I rolled, trying to stem my descent. A rock broke my fall. I slammed into it, my leg wedged in a crevice. When I tried to move, something snapped. I screamed.

A paw slapped over my mouth.

"Easy, little one, it's just me."

Pain filled my world with red hot pincers, the devil's teeth at my leg. I thrashed and giant arms slid around me, clamping me tight.

Pain receded in the face of terror. My eyes rolled like a horse faced with a wolfish predator. The thing was half man, half wolf. It was not real. It was not possible.

A second beast dropped next to me. It wore Vik's loose breeches, the belt with the axe and knives and short sword. But it was grey-furred like a wolf with a white splash on its muzzle.

"Hold her still," the creature growled in Vik's voice. I started in terror, but the hard body behind me kept me from jarring my throbbing leg.

The black monster held me as the grey one clawed the boulders apart. The mist swirled, filling my nostrils with the stench of rotting corpses. I gagged against the black-furred paw and it tucked me more firmly into its body.

"Easy, be still," Thorsteinn's voice crooned. "Vik's almost got you free."

Face buried in the thick pelt, I drew in big gulps of the rich scent. Fur, earth, tangy pine, and a fresh smell like the air after a storm. A paw settled on the nape of my neck. I glanced up—and met Thorsteinn's grey eyed stare.

"How?" I breathed.

The beast's face had a human expression of regret. "Forgive us, little one. We should've told you."

Another wave of mist rolled over us, thick and oily. I hugged the monster's neck, listening to the dreaded slow, steady thump of a hundred undead soldier's marching in lockstep. I gasped. "They're coming closer."

"It'll be all right," Thorsteinn soothed me. To Vik he said, "Hurry."

With a final grunt, Vik broke the rocks holding my leg. Thorsteinn pulled me free. I looked down and almost swooned. My breeches were torn, red lining the seam. Underneath there was a flash of white bone. At the sight, agony shredded me. I gritted my teeth against my cries of pain. I had endured beatings and never cried out. This was no different.

"Broken," Vik reported grimly. "I can set it but..." his hand hovered over my leg. I would've begged him not to touch me, if I could speak.

"There's no time," Thorsteinn snarled. The drumbeat footsteps had grown closer.

I whimpered as Thorsteinn lifted me in his arms. Already his feral looks were less frightening. This was Thorsteinn. My *tortured body recognized him, was drawn to him as it had been from the first, in a way I couldn't explain.*

"Forgive us, little one. We have run out of time." Smoothing back my hair, Thorsteinn reared his head back, baring his teeth. Before I could shout, he snapped and sunk his teeth deep into me, at the tender juncture where my shoulder met my neck. A flash of red as he broke the skin. His hand muffled my scream.

On my left side, Vik ripped open the neck of my jerkin, lifted my hair, and bit. A ferocious sting flashed through me, followed by a glimmer of something else, something wonderful. The pain ebbed and swirled away.

"There," Thorsteinn lifted bloodstained fangs, and I fainted.

I WOKE, *blinking blearily. Strong arms tightened around my body.*

"Thorsteinn?" I mumbled. "Where are we?"

"Safe. high in a tree." He sat cradled in the crook of a giant branch. My legs dangled off his lap, my feet swinging in midair. Far below, the mist swirled around the trunk. "Nothing can touch us here." I shivered, and he palmed the back of my head, steadying me. "How's your leg?"

In a flash it returned—the mist, our route along the hill, the monsters who were really Thorsteinn and Vik. My broken leg, their fangs flashing as they bit me.

With a gasp, I grabbed my neck. The pain was gone. There was no broken skin, no blood, no sting.

"There's still a mark," Thorsteinn told me, faint amusement in his tone. "But the healing worked."

"How—?" I gaped further as I touched my leg. The breeches were still torn.

"That's what the bond does, little one."

I felt it then, a honeyed warmth rushing over me. Two strong cords, one Thorsteinn, one Vik.

"What is this?" I whispered.

"We marked you. You're ours now," He cradled me closer, mouth curving in a rare grin. "You belong to us. No more running, little one."

I stared into his storm grey eyes. I wanted to ask what they'd done. I did not understand but I knew it was magic that joined us together, magic that had healed me. When I opened my mouth, not a protest or a question came out.

"You saved me."

Thorsteinn gazed at me steadily. "Yes."

Ahead, on another branch, Vik set down the knife he'd been sharpening, and waved. I raised my hand in greeting, still filled with wonder.

I did not know these warriors. I did not fully understand their enemy, the Corpse King, or why he targeted the abbey. I did not know what my life would be like as their captive or why, among all the young woman of the abbey, they chose me.

I pressed the tight skin of my leg where the bone had once broken through, marveling. The healing had left no mark. It wasn't even sore. In my blood, the bond hummed.

"You asked my name, once." I swallowed. "Do you still want to know it?"

Thorsteinn's brows quirked as if to say, Of course.

"Sorrel." I told them, sitting high in the tree, my feet waving in the breeze. "My name is Sorrel."

~

Now

.   .   .

"Sorrel. Sorrel."

I woke with the two warriors standing over me. I rolled to a sitting position. I was back in the tree lodge. All that had passed between us—every good memory—paled in light of my sins.

"It's done."

My gaze flitted between them until Vik explained, "The Alphas passed judgment. You are guilty of harming Rosalind."

My hands fisted in the blankets.

"Do you wish to know your sentence?"

I didn't answer. They'd tell me anyway.

Sure enough, Vik squatted close to me. "The penalty for harming a spaewife is death."

So, I'd been told.

"But since you are a spaewife yourself, the Alphas agreed this is a special case." He ran his hand over my head. "They also took into account that we had tried and failed to form a bond."

I flinched and looked away. I did not need to be reminded that I had been used and cast aside.

Gentle hands settled on my shoulders, right over the twin bite marks they'd given me what seemed like so long ago. "Sorrel, it is a good thing. If there is no bond, then there's a chance to redeem you." His large, tattooed hand settled on my shoulder, right above the old bite mark. "To claim you."

I held my breath. Was he saying what I thought he was saying?

"Sorrel, look at me," Thorsteinn ordered, and waited until I raised my gaze.

"They've given us another chance. We have one moon to bind you to us and turn you into our mate."

I frowned, my brow wrinkling.

"The Alphas spared your life," Vik said. "The story we told them worked."

Thorsteinn knelt in front of me, crowding close until all I saw was his stern face. "You are wild and disobedient. A threat to yourself and all others. To save your life, we must prove you are bonded and submit fully to us." His voice was a guttural growl.

I lick my lips and challenged, "And what if you fail?"

Thorsteinn snarled and Vik spoke up. "We will not fail. Sorrel, we're going to tame you."

ik

"No," she raised her head. "You can try. But you will never tame me."

"That is what you think," Thorsteinn growled, and I put a hand on his arm.

"Are you so eager for your own death? You attacked another spaewife. She lies asleep, on the edge of death, and the pack is calling for your blood. If you do not submit to us, your life is forfeit." I motioned to the lodge entrance. "Even now there are warriors prowling the mountain. If they found you unattended, they would snap your neck and not feel remorse."

"Let them come for me," she said fiercely. "I would fight them."

"You would die," Thorsteinn said.

"Sorrel," I started to reason with her and Thorsteinn waved a hand.

"Enough. We will argue with you no longer. You will submit to us. We will teach you to obey. If you do not, you will not like the consequences."

"Do what you will," she hissed. "I will never submit to you."

I squatted close and caught a lock of her hair, tugging on it playfully. "Not even if we make the rewards greater than the punishment?" I caressed her shoulder and her eyes dropped. She flushed. Ah, yes, she was still affected by us. "You remember," my voice grew deeper. "We shared a bond."

"A bond?" She wrenched her shoulder away. "That's not what you told the Alphas."

"We explained why we said that. To save your life. To give you a chance."

"I don't want you anymore." She crossed her arms over her chest. "Have you thought of that?"

"Enough," Thorsteinn said. "You do not trust us. You will in time."

She swallowed, her head bowed so her short hair covered her face.

Do you think this is the way? I asked Thorsteinn.

He jerked his chin up. *Hold. Hold steady.* "Tonight, we begin. First, we punish you for leaving us. For putting our property in harm's way."

"Very well," she muttered.

I raised my brows. Could it be so easy?

"You want to punish me? Fine." She rose and ripped off her jerkin. "Do your worst."

I stifled a laugh. She was still defiant. Still the Sorrel we had fallen in love with from the first.

She turned her back to us, and I sucked in a breath. In an instant, I was across the room and touching the scars on her back. Long white lines on her brown skin. "Who did this to you?"

She whirled, holding up her jerkin between us like a shield.

"You said you wished to punish me." Her chin rose. "What does it matter that someone else already has?"

"Answer me," I growled. I brushed her arms aside. My hands clamped on her shoulders and turned her to face me. "If one of the pack has hurt you, I'll—"

"The nuns," She burst out. "The nuns did it. Back at the abbey."

"Why?" I turned her and ran a hand down her back, brushing every ancient weal. How had I never seen this?

She hid from us. Always. Thorsteinn reminded me. *And we let her. She had suffered trauma both from the Corpse King and us forcing the bond. We thought we would coax her to open to us, in time. And then we ran out of time.*

We made a mistake, brother. We never should have left. I told him, regret filling my voice, choking me. *We never should have accepted that patrol. We should have stayed with her and made sure of the bond. If we have missed our chance—*

It's not too late, Thorsteinn insisted. I was not so sure.

"I never saw this," I said to Sorrel, still tracing the marks. "You hid them well." Always bathing out of sight. Never stripping in front of us. We had thought she was shy. We allowed her to hide.

We had missed so much.

She shivered under my touch but did not draw away.

"Why did the nuns hurt you?" I asked again.

"Because I would not submit. You see, I have never been

good and obedient. Following the rules never gave me anything. The only remedy is to go my own way."

I cupped her chin "You will obey us." I hunkered down to meet her angry gaze. "You will find you enjoy it."

She wrenched away "I will never enjoy it." She backed away and I let her, for now.

"I swear this. We will bring you to heel. But you will find pleasure in it."

"I don't believe you."

"You won't have to believe. You'll know," Thorsteinn said.

"Firm, fair correction," I said. "Nothing that harms you. Just enough of a sting to teach you who is your master."

"You are not my masters," she hissed.

"We are," Thorsteinn strode forward, herding her back to me. Her stiff form bent and swayed. We read it in her posture and her scent—that slight hesitation. The desire to yield.

"It's been a long road, Sorrel." I kept my voice soft. "You don't have to run any more. You don't have to fight."

"We will protect you, little one." The way Thorsteinn towered over her, it seemed ridiculous such a small woman could turn us inside out. Yet she had.

"I do not need your protection," she said, wrapping her arms around herself.

"No? We are all that stands between you and the angry pack." Thorsteinn crossed his arms over his chest. "They call for your blood. Shall we turn you over to them instead?"

"No," I said before she could answer. I drew her close. "We will never let them touch you. Never. We will wrap you in layers of safety, so nothing harms you again."

Emotion rippled across her face. I caught her chin before she could hide.

"Yield to us, Sorrel. I promise it will be worth it. Now

come," I patted my knee. Thorsteinn and I agreed I'd be the first to punish her. Of the two of us, I was more level headed about her attempted escape. Thorsteinn was surprised that she ran. I was not. Women always leave.

"Over my lap," I ordered, smoothing my face of all emotion.

Uncertainty flickered over her face. Confusion. Anger. Stubbornness. She would not bend easily. Good.

"You will lie over Vik's lap and accept your punishment. Or we will march you up the mountain and bind you to a post and whip you for all to see."

She stiffened. *You fool,* I opened the bond between me and Thorsteinn and blasted him. *Did you not see the scars on her back?*

I rose and caught her chin, forcing her to look at me. "We would use a soft flogger. One that leaves marks that fade. Never, ever scar."

"As I told you before," she sneered, even as I felt her pulse fluttering. "Do your worst."

"As you wish." I shrugged and tossed her up over my shoulder. She struggled marginally as I crossed the room and sat, positioning her over my lap. Her breeches tore as I tugged them down.

"What are you doing?" she cried, kicking.

"Punishing you."

"My clothes," she writhed so hard I let her escape.

"You will not need them for a time. Clothes are a privilege you must earn."

"You intend me to go naked in front of the pack?" she clutched her jerkin.

I growled, pulling her close with a hand clamped on the nape of her neck. "Never in front of the pack. We will never share you."

Something flickered across her face. Relief. She hid it behind a sullen frown. "You say it like I'm a possession."

"You are," I announced. "You belong to us. It's time you knew it. You may wear the jerkin for now, if you accept your punishment willingly. Come, back over my lap."

Something flared in her scent. Arousal. Thorsteinn halted his pacing, angling his head towards the scent.

I hid my surprise but not my glee.

"You don't have to act like you're enjoying this." she muttered but pushed herself over my lap.

"I'm not acting. I intend to enjoy every bit of this. Now how many swats for running away?"

She started to answer, and I clapped my hand on her bottom. "Not up to you. I say—as many as it takes to remind you every time you sit."

I squeezed the globes of her tight bottom, warming the flesh. I may have spent an extra-long time doing this, enjoying the scent of arousal that rose like the sweetest perfume. "You are truly a spaewife," I murmured, chuckling at her annoyed huff. "One more thing, little mate. It's okay to cry."

"I don't cry." She ground her teeth.

"If you say so." I palmed her bare ass. "But it will do you good."

"You cry when you get spanked?" She raised her head to glare at me. I could only shake my head at her defiance.

"Careful. Little ones who challenge their mates get fucked. Hard," I slapped the underside of her rounded bottom, enjoying the sharp crack that echoed about the lodge.

Her eyes darted to the floor, but her scent rose around me, a sweet miasma. She could not hide her arousal.

"You like this. Admit it."

"I..." a sigh shuddered through her.

"No matter. You do not have to say it," I delivered three crisp swats to the right cheek, admiring the pink blush. "I can smell it well enough."

Her head tossed back and forth, her brow wrinkled in confusion. She was an innocent. We had not touched her intimately. Why had we waited so long? The space between us was now a chasm.

We wanted to be sure. We claimed her so quickly, to heal her.

Our mistake, brother. We should've done this from the first. Spanked her for running and fucked her until she would never think to leave.

Better late than never.

I hoped so. I hoped it was not too late.

The spanking went on. I paused plenty of times to rub her sore bottom, easing the sting and awakening more feelings in her. It wasn't the pain that would bring her obedience.

Sure enough, I reached between her legs to find her silky lips. "So sweet and wet. Do you know how to touch yourself to feel good?"

A slight sob ran through her.

"Shhh, let it out, there's a good lass."

She pushed away from me, scrambling back.

"Leave me alone."

Thorsteinn started for her and I gestured him to leave her. She could be angry. She could put up walls for now.

One way or another, we'd tear them down.

Will this work? I asked via the bond. Sorrel was curled up on a pile of pelts, sleeping bathed in firelight. Every so often she twitched.

"It must work," Thorsteinn answered out loud, all confidence. He couldn't hide his trepidation from me. I felt his emotions through the bond. "If it does not, the alphas will pronounce her sentence."

She cannot die. Not after everything we have been through.

Before that happens, we will leave. We will take her and run.

I shook my head. *And how long would we survive without help from the pack?* The Corpse King had grown powerful. Even when we were on patrol, we relied heavily on our pack mates to give us aid. Until we rose up together to defeat our enemy, the safest place for any spaewife is on our mountain.

We will train her to obey, Thorsteinn insisted. *Only when she is truly tamed can we ensure her safety.*

I clenched my jaw before I said what I thought: Sorrel would never be tamed.

Thorsteinn caught my hastily banned thought. He glared. *She will break. I will make sure of it.*

Poor little maiden. I crossed the lodge and squatted next to her, tugging a pelt over her shoulders.

Her forehead wrinkled. She had so many burdens, even in sleep. Surely, she would allow us to take at least one.

We must convince her she belongs with us. As we should've from the first, Thorsteinn said.

And if it doesn't work? I traced a finger over her brow, wishing I could smooth the worry lines there.

It must.

We didn't voice what we feared most: we'd waited too long to make Sorrel ours.

∼

SORREL

· · ·

A ROUGH HAND shook me awake in darkness. For a moment I was back in the abbey, getting roused first by my friends, then by an angry nun with a switch.

"Sorrel, time to rise," Vik rasped.

"No. Too early." I tried to cover my head with a pelt, and he pulled it away.

"You must wake," he said with a laugh. "We've got a long day ahead of us."

I raised my head and glared at the darkness beyond the entrance of our tree lodge.

"Rise now, or after a spanking. Your choice."

With a huff, I sat up.

"Good lass," Vik grinned.

"Where is Thorsteinn?"

"Gone to hunt. Come." He tugged me to standing and led me to the far side of the fire pit where a pot of water steamed.

"First a wash." He tugged my jerkin up and I caught his forearms.

"You used to let me bathe myself." They even gave me privacy. Even around my own friends, I refused to undress. The scars on my back were only part of it. I did not want anyone to see me without my armor.

"That was before you ran. Now you will rely on us for everything. Eating. Sleeping. Bathing," his voice deepened. "Pleasure."

I flushed and looked away. They had only begun to initiate me into the rites of pleasure before they were called away on patrol. Still, I remembered.

"You remember it, don't you?" he asked. "How we held you and cared for you?"

"Yes, I remember." I raised my chin. "And then you left."

"That was our folly, and our greatest regret."

I blinked at the sadness in his tone.

"Come," he pulled off my jerkin. I reached for the cloth and he tutted. I gritted my teeth and stood still as he ran the cloth over my neck and shoulders, down my breasts.

"We will wash you every night like this," he informed me in a low tone. "We would've last night, but you fell asleep so quickly."

"I—" last night I'd succumbed to exhaustion after the spanking. "I was tired."

"So you will be every night. We will wear you out," Vik promised with a wicked flash of fang.

I bowed my head. Frowning, he tipped up my chin, "What is it, little one?"

"You say you will claim me. But what if the bonding does not work?"

"It will work. We will not stop until it's complete."

"What if it is not possible?"

"Let us worry about that." He rubbed the cloth between my breasts, slowly washing down my front. I pushed him away, and he tutted at me. "Hands behind your back," he ordered, and slapped the side of my thigh with the cloth when I refused. Rolling my eyes, I did as he bid. The sooner the bath was over, the better.

But not so for Vik. The huge warrior crouched over me, his touch surprisingly gentle. He lingered at the tips of my breasts, chafing them with the cloth until I sighed. His cheek curved, and I fisted my hands to keep from smacking him.

"Funny," he murmured, kneeling and bending to run the cloth between my legs.

"What?" I grabbed his broad shoulders to stay upright. My teeth gritted. I was not affected by his touch. I was not.

"I would've thought you'd fight me by now."

I raised a brow. "You want me to fight?" I asked the top of his head. "I thought you wanted me to obey."

"Not I," Vik's fangs flashed as he smirked, still threading the cloth between my legs. The rhythm never ceased, pressure growing at the apex. Soon it would be too intense for me to ignore.

"Fine then," I drawled. One moment I was still. The next I had thrown myself backwards, kicking the pot and sending it flying. Water splashed everywhere. Even though I hadn't pushed him hard, Vik landed on his back. He roared and I froze like a cornered rabbit, only to realize his howl was laughter. He rose and advanced on me, dripping wet, sloshing through the water pooled on the floorboards. I lost my lead and he lunged, catching me easily. I pounded his back, kneeing him in the side. His body was so hard, I did more damage to myself. We ended up tangled on the pelts. He dropped his long body over mine, pinning my wrists to the floor. Still, I writhed.

"Sorrel," he laughed. "Give up, sweet. Little shield maiden."

"Never!" I kicked upwards, aiming between his legs. At the last moment he turned, and I stubbed my toe on his iron thigh. I yelped and he dropped down, flattening me. "Beautiful," he pronounced, and heat flooded me. His lips found mine and he murmured, "Little fighter. Lovely and fierce."

He kissed me and I bit his lip.

"Yes," he growled, and wrenched my head back by my hair. His lips burned down my jaw, his beard abrading my vulnerable throat. He pinned me with his giant body, lifting enough of his weight on corded biceps that I wasn't crushed.

His hips covered mine, the bar of his erection pressed into my leg.

I don't know when I stopped fighting and started kissing him. At one point he angled his head, coming up for air. Snarling, I gripped handfuls of his hair, wrapping my arms around his broad shoulders and tugging him down. His laughter filled my mouth.

He dragged his thigh between my legs, right over the sensitive junction. Sparks flew up from my aching center.

"Is this what you like?" his voice was heavy in my ear. His body covered mine, arms bracketing my head, long legs stretched over me. His knee rocked slowly, pressing the perfect spot. "Does this feel good?"

"Yes," I arched under him, my nipples furled and needy. "More."

His dark chuckle sent tingles down my back. He continued rocking his thigh between my legs, rubbing me senseless. I moved with the heady rhythm, my feet finding the floor and pressing up, my hips straining for more stimulation. I rubbed myself against Vik's heavy thigh, ignoring his amused laughter. I did not care that Vik was mastering me. I did not care that he was the enemy. I reached for the sensation spiraling higher and higher, desperate for more.

Pleasure broke over me. I gasped and bucked, my feet drumming on the floor.

"Good," he praised me. "Very good, little one."

I blinked and Vik rose over me, unfastening his breeches with one hand.

"Stay there," he ordered and fisted his cock. His eyes burned on my breasts, my legs, my face. Mustering my weak limbs, I started to sit up.

"No," he barked, as stern as Thorsteinn. "Lie still."

It was torture to lie there, my center throbbing, as he

handled himself. The warriors had been careful around me before, giving me plenty of soft touches and sweet words, but never igniting intense desire or driving me inexorably towards pleasure.

I watched, fascinated as his essence spurted from the broad head of his cock, coating my chest.

"Yes," Vik purred. "You will wear our scent. We will mark you this way before you leave this tree."

"We're leaving?"

"Do you not want to train?"

"I thought..." They'd trained me, sparred with me before. But everything had changed. "I thought I was to be punished."

"This is your punishment," He said, taking my hand and running it through his gleaming essence until my skin shone. "To smell like us. To wear our scent. To be driven mad with longing."

My legs clenched. I squirmed, feeling suddenly empty. Rubbing my thighs together lessened the ache.

"That's it," Vik murmured. "That's the way." He pushed my hand between my legs. "Touch yourself."

"I don't... I don't know how."

"You never stroked yourself to completion? Not even at the abbey?"

Biting my lip, I shook my head.

"Let me teach you." He set his thumb against me and stroked upwards with mini movements. "Barely the lightest touch. Do you feel it?"

"Yes," I breathed. All sensation rushed through me, rising to a peak. At the last, he took his hand away.

"Why did you stop?"

"Punishment," Vik smirked and licked his fingers. "I want you weak and wanting us." Laughing he strode across the lodge and tossed a pack back at me. Pleasure time was over, but I was to be left unsated.

I stomped my feet. Vik moved about the lodge, making ready to leave. He was not looking. He told me I might touch myself. Perhaps I could...

The second my hand touched my nether lips, Vik was upon me. "No, naughty one." He planted my wrists on either side of my body and held me easily as I struggled.

"Why?" I shouted.

"This," He freed a hand to slip between my legs, "Belongs to us. You receive pleasure only at our hands or our command."

I thrashed under him, ashamed at how easily he held me. Finally, I stilled.

"Good girl." He rose and pulled me up. "You're learning."

"I'd learn faster if you didn't tease me."

"But I love to tease you," he grinned, then caught my face between his hands. My breath caught at his tender expression. "We will do everything we can to bind you to us."

My body still ached for more stimulation, but his gentle voice soothed the cracked wound of my heart.

"You belong to us, Sorrel. We'll bind you to us forever, so you will never ever leave.

VIK

SORREL'S dark eyes met mine. Lately she'd looked hard and wary, but with her body soft and flushed from her climax, she looked different. Hopeful.

Her skin pearly with my seed. My scent mingled with hers. It pleased the beast.

My chest rumbled with a contented half-growl, I rubbed my cheek against hers, angling my head to brush my beard over her forehead and down her left cheek. As I did, something flicked in the open bond. A light touch, like a butterfly alighting on a flower. Quick and then gone. But it had been there.

A third presence waited in my mind, expectant. I sent my question to Thorsteinn through the bond. *Did you feel that, brother?*

Yes, a touch of hope in him, too. But then, more wary, *What have you done?*

I didn't answer. I teased Thorsteinn too. He wouldn't be pleased I'd touched her without him. But if we'd touched her from the start, maybe we wouldn't be in this predicament.

Sorrel sighed when I released her. Her eyes followed me as I fetched the pack I'd made for her. "Here. Get dressed."

I left her to dress and finished preparing to leave, gathering my weapons, dousing the fire.

When I turned back, she still stood naked, hunched over what I'd given her.

"Sorrel? Is something wrong?"

Her head jerked nay. She remained hunched, was she close to crying? She never cried.

"You replaced them," her chin wobbled.

She held the new tunic and breeches we got her. From the beginning, we knew she didn't like dresses. Breeches were the first gift we'd given her, barely a day after taking her from the abbey.

"Do you not like them? I thought you preferred breeches."

"I do." Her eyes glittered with unshed tears that alarmed me more than a horde of draugr. "You remembered."

"You're a hunter and a fighter. Breeches are far better."

"I know."

"Then what is it? What is wrong?"

"The warriors said I was strange. They would make me wear a dress."

"What warriors? Where?" I would kill them all.

"The nuns, too. They would beat me if I..." she raised the breeches.

I looked from her to the clothes. "The nuns aren't here. If they were..." I left the threat unfinished. I did not like to kill women. But I would, if it meant Sorrel's happiness.

"No one let me wear them. No one," she repeated, intent on my face, "but you."

"Yes, well. They're better for sparring." She was looking at me with the world in her eyes and I couldn't take it. "It wasn't me anyway," I backed away, grabbing my sharpening stone and pocketing it. "It was Thorsteinn. He made sure to raid a village or two and grab some pairs. It was nothing." That wasn't true. The first pair we gave her, yes, was raided. But after that we found someone to make them for coin.

"Come on now," I spoke gruffly. "Put them on. We must be off."

She rushed to put them on as if afraid I'd change my mind.

"If we hurry, there will be time for sparring before Thorsteinn returns. Since you were good, you can climb down."

She gave a small smile at that. She loved her independence. I had to bite my tongue all the way down, worried like an old woman that she might fall. But she wriggled down the trunk like a squirrel and sprang safely to the ground.

"Some of the warriors think that you should be locked up," I told her when we were on the ground. "Caged or chained to a rock, or worse."

She angled her face away, frowning.

"They will not like seeing you roam freely about the mountain. Stay by my side. Close to me, as if bound by a leash."

She made a face and I grasped her chin firmly.

"You obey us, or you will be hobbled."

Her lips pressed together in a sign of rebellion. I chucked her under the chin.

"Obey. It will go easier on you. But if you fight us... it will be more fun."

She frowned thoughtfully all the way to the practice site. We'd set this up soon after we first brought her here, and used it a few times before the thick snows set in. She'd longed to be a warrior and we indulged her, giving her breeches and weapons to wear, letting her cut her hair short. We wooed her in our own way, but whenever we'd touched her, she'd shied away. A result of her capture by the enemy, we thought, and let her be. But the rift only grew, until the three of us lived like warriors, side by side but never closer. By the time we were called to patrol, it seemed easier to go and start over when we returned.

We were wrong. We should have done everything to bind Sorrel to us, make her truly our mate. Touched and teased her until she clung to us. If we'd claimed her properly, when the time came for our patrol, we would've fought not to go. Or at least made it clear that we weren't abandoning her. It was a mistake, leaving her.

Sourness turned my stomach. We would make it up to

her, do anything to bring her closer. Thorsteinn with his strict rules, and me with my touching and teasing and playful methods.

This morning proved she responded to them. I would've kept her there, limp and lissome on the pelts, if I hadn't planned a training day. Of course, plans could change...

"What are we doing here?" Sorrel asked. Outside, she came alive. Her cheeks were flushed and her eyes glowed bright. I ran a hand down her back, and enjoyed her shiver, the anticipation running through her body. Maybe we didn't need to train. There was a patch of soft ground, there, under the hemlocks...

"Vik." Sorrel poked me. I caught her hand and kissed the palm, right at the juncture of her wrist. Another shiver. I touched my tongue to the sensitive spot, enjoying her wriggling a moment before letting her go. That would teach her to poke me.

"You remember your lessons?" I waved a hand around the clearing.

"A little." She frowned and a little line appeared between her brows. "It's been a long time."

Too long. Our fault. "Here," I tossed her my long knife. It stuck in the ground at her feet. "We practice throwing today."

I directed her to throw at the trunk of a dying tree. After a few throws, I stood behind her and corrected her stance, taking every opportunity to run my hands over her body. Her first perfect throw came soon after, and I rewarded her, caressing her chest and collaring her throat to rub my face in her hair. She still smelled like me.

"Why are you doing this?" she asked after I pulled away. Her eyes were bright, her cheeks flushed. After we were done throwing, I decided, I'd prop her on a rock, spread her legs wide, and lick her to completion.

"You'll see." I took out my second knife and tossed it at the tree. It stuck beside hers, quivering, their handles almost touching. We marched together to fetch our respective blades.

"The pack will not like to see a woman armed and fighting."

"If they are upset, it is no concern of mine. They are not your caretakers. We are. Besides," I removed my blade with a quick yank, and she did the same. "If anything upsets them, it will not be your blade work. It'll be the sight of a woman wearing men's clothes." I nodded to her strange attire.

I'll never forget her face when we presented her with the clothes she wished to wear. She grasped them close, her mouth trembling. It was the closest we'd seen her come to crying.

I frowned at that. Had we ever seen her cry? Not even when she broke her leg on that long, awful route from the abbey to the mountain, racing to elude the Corpse King's clutches.

"I know I am a strange sight," she said. "The other spaewives teased me."

"Your friends?" My voice dropped to a growl.

"They are not all my friends."

"I thought you were close with them."

She shrugged. "I tried, but they did not like me. I was different." Her face was carefully blank.

"Because you made a bow and tried to hunt? Because you preferred breeches to dresses and ran from your chores to climb trees."

"Yes," she said distantly. "They used to tell on me."

"And then the nuns beat you."

"And then the nuns beat me. They used switches until it became clear I would not cry out. They hit me hard enough to mark my skin, but I would make no sound. I would not give them the satisfaction. Some of the orphans jeered at me, telling me next time I would cry."

I turned away to hide the sudden flash of rage. "They did not stand by you? One of their own?" I would hunt them down and make them pay.

"Some of the orphans went out of their way to make sure I was punished. The worst was..." She bit her lip.

"Who? Who was the worst?" If Sorrel wasn't speaking of women, I'd challenge them myself. As it were, I might call on them to be punished. Publicly whipped.

"Rosalind."

I sobered at the name. Rosalind was the one who lay unconscious, hit by a stone from Sorrel's sling.

"Is that why you hurt her?"

"No," Sorrel said quickly, but she didn't offer why. She threw her knife and hit the target perfectly, then plucked my own knife out of my hands and threw it too.

Sorrel

I BIT my lip as Vik stalked to the target and wrenched out the knives as if they personally offended him. He returned, but instead of handing me the knives, threw them himself. When I went to fetch them, I struggled because they had sunk so deep.

"Here," Vik's shadow fell over me as I tugged the first

knife free. I staggered back and he steadied me with large hands at my hips. "Let me."

As I grasped the second knife's handle, his hand closed over mine. Together we freed the second knife. He turned me to face him, holding the knife between us.

"If you have an opening to throw the knife, use it. Aim for the torso so you have a better chance of hitting something. Complete the throw and run. Promise me you won't make a stand."

He brushed the hair from my face and cupped my chin.

"Why did Rosalind torment you?"

I tried to turn my face away and he held it still.

"You were both orphans," he peered at my face. "Spaewives collected into the abbey. Why did you not band together, and free yourself?"

"I tried. I wanted us to." I'd told Thorsteinn and Vik of how I learned to hunt and forage while I was at the abbey. I trained myself to live off the land, so one day I might disappear. Find a home in the woods and fend for myself. "I wanted to run away, and I was willing to take my friends."

"Including Rosalind?"

"At first, maybe. But after she betrayed me." I shook my head. "We did not speak, even though I knew she also had plans to leave." Rosalind was one of the girls the friar singled out for attention. I had thought she would join me in planning to escape. Instead, she turned me in to our keepers. After all this time, the betrayal still hurt.

"She was with you in the lodge of unmated spaewives," Vik murmured.

"Yes. She was there." We avoided each other for days before falling into old patterns. The girls were curious why I had been with two warriors all winter. *Where are they now?*

Why did they leave you here? When I hadn't answered, hadn't known how to answer, Rosalind spoke up for me. *Isn't it obvious? The warriors who mated her didn't want her anymore.* Rosalind was the first to vocalize the truth. She laughed at my stunned expression. *It's all right, Sorrel. We're all unwanted here.*

"Did you speak to her?" Vik asked, breaking me from the cruel memory. "Did she have plans to leave?"

I searched his bearded face as he searched mine. "I thought you told the Alphas I led her astray."

He made a frustrated noise. "We told the Alphas what they needed to hear. Now I want to hear from you. You said Rosalind left and you followed. I am trying to understand." His face was earnest.

Vik and Thorsteinn said they wanted the truth. But did they? Thorsteinn thought me wild and demanded my obedience, but Vik... perhaps there was a chance he'd believe me. Even if I couldn't tell him everything.

"Rosalind spoke of leaving the mountain, yes. She was troubled." It felt wrong to speak ill of a woman lying close to death but saying this did not betray her. "The night she left, though, things were... strange."

"Strange? How so?"

"I don't know," I whispered. How could I describe what I only felt? "It was dark, but the moon gave me enough light to see. I raced after Rosalind, but she always stayed far ahead. I followed her golden hair. There were patrols, but..." I shook my head. "The mists obscured us. Rosalind and I walked through the mists and it was almost as if the warriors couldn't see us."

Vik's face was blank. I ducked my head. "I told you it was strange."

"Yes," he said slowly. "But stranger things have

happened. Sorrel—do you think magic was somehow involved?"

"I don't know. I just felt I had to catch up with Rosalind. I felt it was my fault that she left. I had spoken of wanting escape. I didn't think she'd be brave enough to try it." I spoke to my feet, miserable. "So, you see, when you told the Alphas I led her astray... it was true."

"You feel guilty because she left of her own accord?"

"Yes. It is my fault. She left, and now she's hurt. It's all my fault."

"Not from what you've told me," Vik said slowly. "It sounds like there were other forces at play. Sorrel, what happened after you left the mountain?"

I shook my head. "You know what happened."

"I know you and Rosalind left the mountain. I know the Berserkers found you both, her unconscious with a wound on her temple, you standing over her with a sling. I want to hear your version."

"What does it matter?"

"What you have to say matters to me."

I pressed my lips together and he nudged me. "Tell me, Sorrel. I will listen."

He would listen, but could I tell him what I suspected? That Rosalind had been in league with the Corpse King, and I had to stop her before it was too late.

"I didn't want to hurt Rosalind," I said finally. "I had to. To save our lives."

"What?" His head cocked. "What do you mean? To save your lives... were you in danger?"

If I told him anymore, I would name Rosalind a traitor. I couldn't do that. If she lived, she'd wake to face the Alphas' wrath. If she died, I couldn't lead the pack to think she was a traitor.

With a sigh, I hung my head.

"It's no use," a harsh voice rang out behind us. Vik sighed as Thorsteinn stalked into view. The grey eyed warrior arched a brow as he stared down his nose at me. "She will not tell us the truth."

He was right, but it was no longer a matter of will. I wanted to tell them. I touched my lips, willing them to move.

Anger heated my body, but I didn't argue. This was my penance for harming Rosalind. Let everyone believe what they wanted to believe.

THORSTEINN

SORREL TURNED FROM ME, her jaw tight. Her dark hair fell across her face, a veil between us.

Did you have to interrupt? Vik tossed his knife at me. It bounced off my bare chest, handle first, which is how I knew he wasn't trying to kill me. Not that a simple knife throw can kill a Berserker. I retrieved the knife and tested the blade against my palm. The sharp edge sliced a stinging red line across my rough and calloused skin. It healed immediately.

"Was I wrong?" I asked aloud. "Sorrel, did you have something to say?"

"No. Nothing."

I raised a brow at Vik. *See? She does not trust us.*

She never will if you taunt her.

You taunt her all the time.

That's different. He held up his hand, silently ordering me to throw his knife back. I let it fly at a mark just past him and he plucked in out of the air. *She likes it when I tease her. What you say hurts her.*

Regret bit me. I pushed it away. *I don't care, as long as she obeys.* Out loud I said, "Time to put your hunting skills to work. We need meat." I unstrapped a bow and sheath of arrows from my back and tossed them at Sorrel's feet.

She picked them up, examining them carefully. I saw the glimmer of excitement on her face, even as she tried to hide it. "I thought you were hunting," she said, slipping the strap over her shoulder.

"I was," I said. "But not for meat. Come on." I started into the forest. Something whizzed by my face and stuck in the tree trunk. An arrow, the feathered fletch quivering an inch from my face.

I turned on my heel and glowered, shoulders hunched like I was going to pounce. Sorrel met my eyes, glare for glare. Calmly, she plucked the bowstring. "It still works," she explained. If I wasn't so angry I wanted to spank her, I'd be proud.

Vik was laughing like he was drunk. "You're the one who armed her."

"You're the one who taught her how to shoot." I included him in my glare, and he laughed harder.

"He did not," Sorrel protested, her black brows knitted together. "I taught myself. There were days at the orphanage I had to eat what I hunted, or I wouldn't eat at all. And I shared with the orphans who were denied food."

Vik stopped laughing. "They were cruel to you," he growled. "We should've razed the place to the ground when we had the chance."

"It's gone now," Sorrel said, but her face still held the pain of a thousand horrible memories. "The Corpse King destroyed it, and everyone perished. That's what the

Berserkers told me and the other unmated spaewives. All the nuns died. All but Juliet."

"They got what they deserved," I growled.

"Perhaps." Head bowed, Sorrel marched past me. One stride and I caught up to her. It took two of her steps to match my one.

"You do not think they got what they deserved. They mistreated you."

"I was used to it," she said simply. "At least, they never promised to care for me, then abandoned me all the same."

I stepped in front of her, halting her in her tracks. "We never abandoned you."

"You dropped me at the lodge of unmated spaewives. And then you left."

"We planned to return."

"And do what?"

"And keep you." I tapped the underside of her chin, tilting it up. She still didn't meet my eyes. I did not like the blank, distant look in hers. "Claim you."

"You didn't want me. They teased me for it, and I finally understood."

"Who told you that? Who teased you?"

"It doesn't matter. All that matters is you left."

"We returned."

"After it was too late." She jerked away and took a step.

I blocked her path. "It is not too late," I snarled. "You belong to us. You will submit. You will yield."

She didn't reply. She didn't have to. Defiance was written on her face.

"You will yield," I promised her, and stepped out of her way.

3

S *orrel*

WE SPENT the rest of the day hunting while the sun sank slowly. Thorsteinn and Vik used throwing knives and I proved more than a match with my bow. At last we headed home with the bodies of small game strung on a stick propped on Vik's shoulder.

I felt like game myself, tied and trussed between two warriors. They hadn't done anything to make me submit but their presence reminded me

Especially, when, suddenly, Thorsteinn pushed me behind a boulder, and pressed me down. "Kneel," he whispered harshly. I glared but he wasn't looking at me.

"Other warriors," Vik murmured, and I understood. I wasn't supposed to be tromping around woods, happy and free. I was supposed to be locked up in a cage or thrown in a pit, or whatever counted as punishment.

I sank down behind the rock and tucked my knees against my chest.

"Stay," Thorsteinn ordered, like I was a pet. He disappeared before I could snap at him. The wind brought shouted greetings and snatches of conversation. I waited listening. Is this how it was to be? Never allowed to roam on my own. Forced to hide so no one looked on my despised face. So far Thorsteinn and Vik's punishment proved very light. But what sort of life would I have if I stayed and bonded with them? Would I ever be able to mingle with the pack or my friends? No one believed I had done no wrong. Crouched behind the stones, listening for scraps of conversation, I had to conclude my own warriors were ashamed of me.

I crept around the boulders, trying to get a better view. The wind picked up, carrying a pleasant sound—a lighter voice raised in song. It came from behind me. Ducking to stay hidden by the rocks, I dashed behind a line of bushes and crawled until I could stand. Beyond a briar thicket, a woman's shape rose and bent. A spaewife, toiling over a garden with a hoe. She stood and wiped her brow with a sun browned arm, and I recognized her.

"Hazel," I whispered. "Hazel."

She startled, raising her hoe like a weapon. That almost made me smile. She had always been one of the bravest orphans.

She peered into the bracken. When she saw me, her eye grew round. "Sorrel? You are here? Are you in hiding?"

"Not anymore. I was caught. My guards are close." I jerked my thumb back towards Thorsteinn and Vik, hoping they hadn't noticed me gone.

"Are you all right? My mate said you were almost taken by the Corpse King. Again." She seemed concerned. Maybe she hadn't heard of my crimes. Or maybe she just believed I wouldn't do something so awful without good reason. "What happened?" She pushed her hair off her face, leaving a dark smudge of dirt.

I shouldn't tell her the truth. But then, I couldn't repay her worry with lies.

So I told her the truth. "Rosalind left the mountain. I ran after her."

"Truly?" Her eyes grew even wider. "Why would she run?"

"I don't know." I had my suspicions, but best keep to what I knew.

Hazel bit her lip and looked away. I knew what she was going to ask before she said, "They are saying you killed her."

A flash of painful horror. "Is she dead then?"

"Not yet. Sorrel, what happened?"

I scooted closer so the wind wouldn't carry our voices. "I cannot tell you. I cannot. Maybe if she wakes..."

"Tell me one thing," Hazel's eyes bore into mine. "Did you try to kill her?"

"No." It felt so good to answer. Hazel was the first to ask me outright, instead of assuming.

"But you did hit her?"

"I had to, Hazel. You must believe me." *Please, believe me, when no one else will.*

A pause, and she jerked her head decisively. "I do."

"Sorrel?" A rough, distant voice called. Vik.

"I must go," I whispered, and wriggled backwards through the brush without saying more.

Crouching, Hazel called softly after me. "Be safe, my friend."

I wriggled back the way I'd come. I reached my spot by

the boulders a moment before Vik poked his head around and beckoned.

"Come."

"Are we still going to hunt?" I straightened, brushing dried leaves off my jerkin, hoping he wouldn't notice.

"Of course." Grasping my hand, he lengthened his stride until I ran alongside.

"You think it wise?" Ahead, Thorsteinn waited on the path. He'd clapped the visiting warriors on the shoulder, almost friendly, but now he wore a scowl. "Doesn't the pack want to see me punished?"

"Oh, we told them you were locked in a cage too tight to move," Vik said.

I sucked in a breath, but then he winked at me and I knew he jested.

"I can bear a cage," I informed him. "It would be a nice rest."

"There'd be no rest for you in the cage I have in mind," he murmured with dark glee. "But it would not be punishment. Only pleasure."

"What sort of cage is that?" I stopped short on the path, and he chuckled, pushing me along.

"Misbehave and you'll see. And as for the pack, let us worry about them," he spoke in a louder tone as we reached Thorsteinn. "If you stay close, and do as we bid, you'll be all right."

"Disobedience has consequences," Thorsteinn intoned, and I almost stuck my tongue out at him.

The rest of the day, we spent hunting, only stopping to eat and drink, and fill our waterskin at the stream. Either we were in a secluded corner of the mountain, or Thorsteinn had warned his packmates off, but we saw no one but birds and squirrels and rabbits.

"You're good with the bow," Thorsteinn told me after I brought down three squirrels with a clean shot to the head. I flushed at his serious compliment. "You have skill."

"I practiced," I told him shortly. He ran his hand over my short hair thoughtfully.

"I remember you telling us you had plans to escape the abbey, live in the wild."

"I did. I had my own bow and arrows, and boots and breeches I'd made." I tromped to pick up my last kill and handed it to Vik to secure on the string. "I hoarded supplies and hid them from the nuns."

"Is that why you were beaten? Did they find them?"

"No." I shuddered to think what the nuns would have done if they'd found my stash. Probably locked me in the dark stillroom or the empty well. I still had nightmares from those punishments levied when I was younger. Everyone knew I feared being locked in the dark. That's why I hid my things in the stillroom—no one would believe I would return to the site of my worst punishment. "They punished me for other things."

"Such as?"

I shrugged. "Anything they wanted. I never behaved."

Thorsteinn started to comment, when a signal from Vik made him haul me behind a tree.

"Boar," he mouthed and pointed to a huge shape lumbering at the base of a chestnut tree. At his nod, I notched my bow.

"You must kill it quick. It's a huge one. I did not know there were any of this size left on the mountain." He smiled. "Thor smiles on us this day."

Peering out from the pine, I raised my bow and took aim. A flowering bush blocked a clean shot. I kept sighting down the bow, waiting for the boar to move.

"Patience," Thorsteinn murmured.

I gritted my teeth. My arrows were more suited to hunting small game, but if I could make a killing shot... I waited, tension growing every second. If I killed it, what would I prove? I was a good shot? Would the warriors praise and be proud of me? For a moment the boar blurred, and Rosalind stood in its place. My fellow orphan. She was cruel to me, and I avoided her, but we were still more alike than different. The girls I'd grown up with were the only family I'd known. Even if Rosalind tormented me, she was still like a sister to me.

I hadn't wanted to hurt her. It wasn't my fault. I hadn't run. I had only followed her, wanting to save her. I'd tried to convince her to come home. She'd ignored me, marching on. I hadn't left her.

She'd gone straight to the Corpse King, and I had followed. I'd even helped her. Did that make me a traitor like her?

My arms grew heavy. I dropped the bow.

"I can't," I croaked. I had hit Rosalind. In the end I hadn't protected her at all.

"What's wrong, little warrior?" Thorsteinn's hand stroked the back of my neck.

"Tell us. We will listen."

"I did it," I whispered. "I tried to kill my friend. I didn't want to, but she gave me no choice."

"It was self-defense?" Vik asked.

I bit my lip, wanting to say yes. Not knowing how I could without naming Rosalind a traitor.

Suddenly, I couldn't bear the quiet. Raising my bow, I loosed an arrow. It flew blindly and only the boar's bellow of rage told me it struck.

Thorsteinn thrust me behind him. "Stay out of sight," he

ordered. The boar thrashed and stomped, tearing through the flowered bush and destroying it. It was headed our way.

Cursing, Thorsteinn pushed me. "Run!"

I started to flee but looked back. Thorsteinn stood firm, facing the boar. He would stop the boar or get gored trying. While I ran. I was a coward.

With shaking arms, I raised my bow and took aim. The boar charged. Thorsteinn stood firm. His figure became Rosalind's, the boar a dark skeletal menace, clothed in mist... If I missed my shot, I'd hit Rosalind. I didn't want to hit her. Did I?

"Sorrel!" Thorsteinn shouted, bringing me back to the light filled clearing. There was no mist, no skeleton. Just Thorsteinn and a boar so large, the ground shook under its pounding hooves. "Sorrel, go!"

Why was he shouting at me? The boar was almost upon him. "Look out!" I shrieked.

With a whoop that stopped my heart, Vik broke from the bush. Axe glinting in the sun, he fell on the boar. The great beast turned, tusks tossing. Distracted, it narrowly missed Thorsteinn. Vik leapt onto its back. The great pig roared, and Vik laughed like a madman, digging his axe into its bristled hide.

Thorsteinn waded in, sending a short spear into the beast's side. The two warriors fell on it, hacking at its neck. I shrank further into the shadows between the pines.

Dropping my bow and arrows, I ran. I'd done wrong again. Another failure. Another sin on my head. I was crushed with the weight of them.

I ran until the land sloped and I slid. I grabbed at the surrounding branches to slow my skidding descent. At last, the trunk of a hearty bush bent and held in my grip. Just in time. I came to a scrambled stop at a rocky ledge. Nothing but blue sky and a deadly drop.

Heart pounding, I leaned out. The slope ended abruptly. Below lay a long, sheer cliff. No wonder no one came to this side of the mountain. There was no need to patrol when any assaulting enemy was bound to fall to their death.

But if someone slight and small and good at climbing were to make her way down, there'd be no one to stop her from running.

"Sorrel," the rough cry met my ears. My warriors searching for me. I wriggled back up the slope and picked leaves from my jerkin as I walked back to Vik and Thorsteinn.

They left you. A voice grated, picking at a tiny loose end of my faith, unraveling it. I heard it often at the lodge of the unmated spaewives. Rosalind never ceased her torment.

The boar hung upside down from a tree, ready to be turned into meat.

"Sorrel," Vik stuck his axe into a tree trunk and came to me, stopping before he ran a bloody hand over my head. "You're unhurt."

"I ran," I said. "I'm sorry I wasn't more help—"

"You did well," Thorsteinn said. "I told you to run."

"Yes." But I still felt like a coward.

"We should not take her on the hunt," Vik said, crouching to wipe his hands on the leaves. "It is too dangerous."

"Sorrel did well," Thorsteinn regarded me with granite eyes. What did he see?

I shivered and wrapped my arms around my body. Vik dropped a pelt over my shoulders and wrapped it around me, fussing like a girl dressing her doll.

"We'll carve up the boar, soon. In the meantime, we'll build a fire. Can you help, little warrior?"

I nodded

"Stay close to us. We have called some of the pack to help us transport the meat. It would not do for you to cross paths with them."

Miserably, I agreed.

While the warriors prepped their kill, I wandered through the trees, gathering sticks. Vik and Thorsteinn discussed cooking the meat here. Perhaps they'd build a giant bonfire and celebrate their hunt. Call their warrior brothers to drink and eat. Would they first have to tie me to a tree, like a disobedient dog? I would not be welcome by the pack's fire.

I was not welcome anywhere. Wandering out of the warriors' sight, I let my armful of kindling drop. My head ached. So did my body, with old, remembered punishments. It would be good to lie down and pretend.

I'd wandered into a patch of mist. Cold and thick, it reminded me of the Corpse King's fog. It was such a relief to lie down and close my eyes and pretend to be nothing. Pretend to be dead.

A crow cawed nearby. I rolled and realized how close I was to the cliff's edge. So many people's problems would disappear when I did.

I lay back on the comforting ground. The mist flowed over my face, covering me like a death shroud. Vik and Thorsteinn would be busy skinning the boar, preparing it for transport. At some point they'd come searching for me, but I couldn't face them. Suddenly, all I could think of was escape.

Gripping the bush tight, I leaned out. It wouldn't take much. Just a careful descent. With the right handholds, a light body could climb down the cliff. The Berserkers could not follow fast enough to catch me.

I could be free. And they wouldn't have to bother with me. They could choose another mate. It hurt to think of it, but I'd be long gone. I had the skills to survive the wild. Ironically, the warriors had taught me the skills I'd need most.

And if I met my death, so be it. No one wanted me anyway.

Sorrel, a voice whispered in my head. The merest brush of consciousness, like a light streaming in through cracks in a door. Before it could entice me, I slammed the door shut.

Time to leave.

I wriggled down the hill, escape on my mind. The mist flowed around me, twin white streams. I caught a whiff of rot—

The shadowed skeleton reached out a hand—I drew my sling—

I sat upright. I was on the cliff ridge, my legs dangling over the edge. Why was I here? My head ached.

Jump over... The sinister whisper echoed in my ears. But that could not be right, I did not want to die. All I'd ever wanted was to live my life in peace. A secluded hut deep in the wilderness. Away from everyone.

Climb down...

The wind whistled between the rocks. Far below my feet, the mist gathered, thick as a cloud. I rubbed my head. I could not be thinking of climbing down. Not from this height. It would be certain death.

I pulled myself back. The mist coiled behind me, a snake ready to strike.

You cannot go back. Thorsteinn and Vik will never want you.

I curled in on myself, pressing a hand to my breastbone

to counteract the pain. The voice was right. I could never be the mate they deserved. My only recourse was to escape. Now. Down the cliff. The mist will show me the way.

Holding a root, I extended a leg to find the first foothold...

The root broke and I scrambled, digging my hands into the loam. For a moment, my feet kicked in the air. I lost my grip and with a yelp, I dropped—

And landed on a protruding stone. The wind whistled around me, but I was safe, until I poked my head out to gauge the rest of the way and became dizzy.

Go slowly. Don't be stupid. Fine things to think when suspended over a deadly drop. This whole enterprise was stupid. What had possessed me to run in the first place?

Worthless, another voice hissed. *Run before they do you harm. You aren't wanted anyway.*

Another memory, fighting out of the mist. *Come to me.* A skeletal hand beckoning, but not to me. To Rosalind. The mist surrounded us, seeping into our bones.

The Corpse King became powerful, the warriors had told me. The mountain was warded, but I had faced the enemy twice. Could I be sure what was in my own head?

No. Not if I was hanging half off a cliff. It was shameful, how easily I succumbed to the Corpse King's lies.

Now I had to pull myself back up. An easy task when compared to explaining myself to my warriors.

My feet scraped the stones. While searching for a toehold, my balance shifted. The rock under my hand came loose. I yelped and pressed myself to the rock face. My feet dug into the rock, trying and failing to find footholds. My left hand had the only secure hold, but even that was slipping. When it did, there would be nothing to keep me from plummeting to my death.

The wind picked up and cut through me, cold slicing like knives. The stone scraped my cheek. I was so stupid. I had done this, run again. Why?

The mist, the thought tugged me. *You lay down and the mist covered you. The same mist that surrounded you and Rosalind.*

Stranger things have happened. Vik had said. I heard his voice now, as if he stood behind me and spoke in to my ear. *Sorrel—do you think magic was somehow involved?"*

If I lived through this, I would tell them the truth, I promised myself. I would tell them everything.

But first I had to live...

A huge hand came out of nowhere and ripped me away from the cliff wall.

My captor pulled me aloft. I came face to face with a monster. Black, with a splash of silver on its elongated snout. Thorsteinn. And he was angry, his golden eyes burning me.

I opened my mouth and he roared. My hair blew back from my face and I shut my mouth. Now was not the time to explain.

He dragged me back to the campfire where Vik waited, arms crossed on his chest. I ducked my head so I didn't have to meet his eyes.

Sorrel, the voice came again. It was definitely Vik's. I'd heard him along with the Corpse King. Was I going mad?

Vik crouched and looked me carefully in the eye.

"She's in shock. What happened?"

"I caught her making her escape. Climbing off a cliff."

"I wasn't leaving," I protested. "I started to, but then I realized it was futile and stopped."

"Not soon enough," Thorsteinn snarled and I winced.

"We know you wish to escape. To run. But we cannot tolerate you putting yourself in harm's way."

I didn't wish to escape, though. Not until I'd heard the Corpse King's treacherous voice. Here with the warriors it all became clear. "I'm sorry. About everything."

"We know," Vik murmured. "Sorrel, can you tell us what happened?"

"It was the mist," I said. "The mist made me feel... heavy. It confused me."

"Did it?" Vik murmured.

"I think I know what we're dealing with," Thorsteinn growled. He was fully man again, gathering his hair behind his head and braiding it. "The Corpse King has many weapons."

"The mist told me—" I stopped.

"Go on," Vik prodded me gently.

"It told me you don't want me. That it was better for me to run... and die..."

"Listen well," Thorsteinn was over me in a second, snarling, "You belong to us."

I knotted my hands in my lap. "You can't wish to keep me."

"You believe lies," Vik insisted. "The Corpse King is in your head, and he twists your thoughts. but he is not strong enough to defeat you."

"We thought he put up walls between us, but in truth the walls are yours. And we will breach them, one way or another. Together we will tear them down."

He and Vik exchanged glances before stiffening.

I heard it then, the crack of a branch in the woods. Someone was coming towards us, and not bothering to be quiet about it.

"Incoming," Vik warned.

"They cannot see her like this," Thorsteinn brushed at my clothes. I looked like I'd been rolling down a hillside—which I had.

"Time to put on a show. You can do that for us, right, little wolf?" Vik caught my chin, something in his expression pleading.

"Yes?" I looked from one warrior to another. What was I agreeing to?

"Then fight me," Thorsteinn growled, and pounced.

The flock of Berserkers came upon us wrestling, Thorsteinn clad in a torn jerkin and breeches from his Change, me wriggling like an eel to escape him. Vik greeted the visiting warriors. Sure enough, they all glared at me. One I recognized from his visits to the lodge.

"Jarl, you did not have to leave your post."

"I wanted to see how you fared with your charge," Jarl said.

I forgot for a moment to fend off Thorsteinn and he pounced, lifting me by the back of my jerkin, like a kitten carried by the scruff of its neck. Nose to nose with Thorsteinn, I dangled in his hold. "You will do as we order," he growled.

"I am not your pet." My old angry litany was easy to repeat, but now I had to stifle a smile.

"Oh," Thorsteinn pretended to fume, "but you are."

"I see she is not quite tamed," Jarl said.

"No. But it is better when they fight," Vik drawled. "We enjoy it."

Holding Thorsteinn's gaze, I kicked. He twisted to avoid a blow to his sensitive parts, dropping me. I rolled to my feet and scampered off.

"Enough," Thorsteinn thundered but I kept running, only to find my feet dancing in air as he snatched me back.

"Enough," he closed his teeth around my earlobe and bit gently. I went limp in his arms, only to stiffen as he carried me back to the group of warriors.

"I would think you might tire of such a troublesome mate," Jarl was saying.

"No," Thorsteinn plopped me down and gripped my shoulders to keep me in front of him. "We let her go once. Never again."

"I have a message for her from a spaewife," Jarl said.

I sucked in a breath but kept staring at my feet. If I looked up at Jarl, he might think I was challenging him. Thorsteinn and Vik would protect me, but they would not be pleased.

"What message?" Vik growled.

"Juliet sends her greetings," Jarl said. I felt his gaze crawl over me. "And this: 'Forgive me. It was my fault.' Tell me, Sorrel," Jarl squatted to make me face him. "Why would Juliet say such a thing?"

"That is not for Sorrel to answer," Thorsteinn pulled me back against him. "Surely that is a question for Juliet."

"Sorrel knows. She is keeping secrets," Jarl pointed his finger at me like a spear.

"That is our concern, not yours."

"Not if I go to the Alphas and demand that Sorrel be questioned."

"You do that," Vik warned, "And we will insist that Juliet be questioned as well."

Jarl snarled at that. He cared for Juliet. "Juliet did nothing wrong. We will make Sorrel talk."

"You'll not lay a hand on her. She is ours to deal with," Thorsteinn rumbled.

"And are you dealing with her? She is not cowed or contrite. I do not see signs of punishment."

"Do you not? I will show you how we deal with her disobedience." Thorsteinn turned me to face him, and our play acting began again. "You ran from me."

I bared my teeth at him and growled like an animal. Vik ran a hand over his beard to hide his grin, but Thorsteinn remained stern.

Still holding me fast, he unbent an arm ring from his right bicep. "Time after time we give you a chance to prove your obedience, and time after time you defy our protection," he intoned, "This mountain is full of warriors who want you dead. If you will not acknowledge us as your Masters, we will bind you and force you to obey until you do."

"But—" I protested, and quieted when he shook me.

"You insist on behaving as a wild animal?" He held up the silver ring. "Very, well. We will treat you as one." Wrenching the arm ring open, he curved it around my neck. "Now a chain."

I opened my mouth to protest but Thorsteinn fixed me with a glare.

"Jarl," Vik drawled, holding out his hand. I understood then. The Berserker had come to us with a chain to bind me with. Thorsteinn would be sure they used it—but only my warriors would touch me.

Jarl handed off a long length of iron links. Vik bent the last link open with his fingers and Thorsteinn took it and fastened it to the arm ring. When they stepped back, I wore the silver band around my neck attached to a chain. A collar and a leash.

Thorsteinn backed up. "Come," he ordered, and tugged the leash. This was too far.

Trust us, Vik's voice whispered.

I went to grab the chain and Vik collected my hands

behind me. "Touch it and I will bind your hands behind your back."

"I am not a dog to be led like this," I hissed.

"No," Vik murmured. "But you are our possession. And if you insist on acting like a wild wolf, we will make you our pet."

Thorsteinn snapped his fingers. "Come."

I had to admit the watching pack members looked impressed by my treatment. I fell into step behind Thorsteinn, hoping he would not lead me like this all the way home.

4

S *orrel*

WE HEADED HOME, Thorsteinn pulling me by the leash, Vik taking up the rear. When we reached the great tree, they set me right in the basket. Only when I was in the tree lodge did Thorsteinn unleash me. I waited for him to remove the silver ring from around my neck, but he left it, saying, "I want you wearing something of us."

"But—"

Thorsteinn bent and kissed me. "You did well." He rubbed his stubbled face against mine. "I know that was not easy."

I let out a shaky sigh.

Vik rose from building the fire, dusting his hands. He went to the rope ladder and disappeared.

"He goes to collect our portion of the boar meat. The warriors we called took it away."

"Will it always be like this?" I touched the ring around my neck, but he knew what I meant.

"For a time. But the pack will see you mated to us and forgive you." He ruffled my hair. "One day, it will be all right."

My shoulders slumped. Back at the cliff, I had vowed to tell them the truth, but even if I did who would believe me? The pack certainly wouldn't. Vik and Thorsteinn could shout my innocence from the mountain, and they'd be reviled like me.

Vik and Thorsteinn didn't deserve such a troublesome mate.

"You should send me away," I told him.

"Never." Thorsteinn tipped up my chin, eyes flashing. "Why do you think we would abandon you?"

"You already did, once."

"We told you we would return. But I see," the longer he looked at me the more his hand softened. "It was a long lonely winter. We did not know the spaewives would torment you. We thought there would be some comfort." Leaning forward, he rubbed his stubbled cheek on mine. "Do you know why we stayed away so long?"

I shook my head.

"It takes everything in us to restrain the beast. And when we are with you, Sorrel," his voice deepened, "I fear we are at the end of our control. There were days, whole moons we retained our monstrous shape." The firelight glittered in his eyes, there was a sudden wind, that bore with it the scent of the air after a fierce storm. A moment later it died away.

"But we should have told you. We should've claimed you long before now."

"Why didn't you?" The regret in his voice made me brave. This softer, gentler Thorsteinn I did not have to fight.

"We thought we had," he traced the mark on my right shoulder. The skin still bore the red scar of his bite. "When it became clear you were lost to us, distant, it was too late. We could not restrain the beast." His hand dropped to rub my back, soothing.

"Ho," Vik called as he appeared at the entrance with a pot. Thorsteinn went to help him. I joined them around the fire, reaching for my portion.

"No," Thorsteinn pulled me into his lap. "I will feed you."

I put up a token struggle until he snapped his fingers, his features growing stern. "You will take the food from my hands. Each meal will remind you who cares for you. You rely on us for every bite."

"I am not your pet."

"Are you not?" he asked, his voice deepening. "You are whatever we say you are. If we wish you to crawl and go about on all fours, we will order you."

"Is that what you want? To see me humbled? Groveling? Begging for each bite?"

"Oh, you will beg," Thorstein promised. "But not for food. We will train you to desire our touch. You will desire us above anything, and we will claim you thoroughly."

My breath came unsteadily, but I raised my chin, my stubborn expression answering him.

We stared at each other.

Thorsteinn dipped his head close to mine. "You cannot win this battle of wills. You will accept food from my hand and sit either on my lap or on your knees at my side. Choose."

"Lap," I snapped, and crossed my arms to show my disapproval. When he brought my portion to my lips, I ate hungrily.

"There, that is not so hard," he murmured. "It is easy to submit."

I wanted his words to spoil the meat in my stomach, but my body would not obey. It was happy enough to sit in the big warrior's lap and suck the juices off his fingers until Thorsteinn's eyes flared with heat. Across the fire, Vik chuckled.

After the meal Thorsteinn wouldn't let me up. He washed my hands and face with a wet cloth, then swung me out and set me over his knees.

"What is this?"

"Time for the punishment you earned," Thorsteinn said, holding me down with a huge hand on my back. The other pulled down my breeches. I kicked, but it was no use.

"Vik told you there will be a reckoning every night."

"Every night!"

"Yes," he caressed my bottom thoughtfully. "Though I doubt you will complain about it."

I cursed him, and he answered with a flurry of crisp smacks against my bare bottom. The sound echoed around the lodge, interspersed with Vik's laughter.

"Tell me, Sorrel, do you yield?"

"Never," I growled, and tried to bite Thorsteinn's leg. The warrior shifted me off balance and continued spanking me.

"This is only a warm up," he informed me. "Run from us again, and you'll get much worse."

Worse? My bottom throbbed. When he stopped to rub it, and it was hot as coals against his hand.

I stopped fighting and let my head hang down, my hair covering my face, which was as red as my behind. Especially when Thorsteinn moved his hand to check between my legs.

"See how wet she gets?" Vik murmured. "There's some part of her that needs it."

"Is that so?" Thorsteinn stroked his fingers over my sensitive nether lips lightly, then with more intent. "This is how we will tame you, Sorrel." His fingers kept strumming. "Feeding you. Caring for you. Claiming you."

My legs trembled as the sensation within me grew to a fever pitch.

"No," I burst out. I threw myself off his lap and he let me, astonished.

"Do not touch me this way. Be cruel. Lock me away, but don't touch me that way."

Vik picked me up off the floor.

"Hush, Sorrel." My insides throbbed, need filling every corner until I writhed in torment. "You're safe with us. This is not punishment like the nuns gave you. Let your mates love you. Let us care for you."

"I can't," My voice cracked. I did not cry. I could not. No matter how much I hurt, tears never fell. "I ruined everything."

"No, little one—"

"You don't know," I burst out. "Rosalind lies dying because of me. Because of me."

Vik rubbed my back, soothing me, telling me to let it out.

"It's my fault. I dreamed of leaving the mountain, but not like that."

"You told me things were strange," Vik said, and repeated what I'd told him to Thorsteinn.

"There was mist the night we left," I said. "And later, when..." I'd promised myself I'd tell them the truth of what happened with the Corpse King. But when I opened my mouth, it was like a hand around my throat, strangling me.

"Sorrel?" Vik's hand stilled on my back. "Is something wrong."

I swallowed. "I—" But again my words stuck in my throat, choking me. My hands flew to my neck and lips.

"Sorrel," Thorsteinn crouched in front of me. His worried face filled my vision. "Be easy. Try to breathe."

I gasped as Vik pounded on my back.

"What was that?" I finally asked.

"I'm beginning to wonder..." Thorsteinn began thoughtfully, "if someone laid a spell on you to prevent you from telling the truth."

"A geas?" Vik demanded. "Like in the stories?"

I kept still, my hands at my throat. All this time, I had been afraid to speak because I didn't want to name Rosalind a traitor. Or I'd thought no one would believe me. Could it all be magic?

"It makes sense," Thorsteinn said, coming to me and tipping back my head to search my face. A low growl sounded in his chest the whole time. "I do not like this. Someone has meddled with our bond and our mate." He jerked back and stalked to the end of the lodge, muttering, "I need an enemy I can see. This is not something I can fight."

I felt so tired. After all I'd been through, the enemy was in my own mind. "So there's no use in trying to save me?"

"Sorrel," Vik started, and I wrenched myself out of his grasp.

"You should let me go," I scrambled to my feet. "I am wicked and unruly and now cursed. You should choose another mate." I staggered blindly to the door.

And found myself midair, flying to the bed of pelts. I landed on the soft pile, shocked. Vik was on me in an instant, pinning my arms and legs to the floor.

"No," he ground out in a voice like thunder. "You belong to us, Sorrel, and we won't let you go."

*V*IK

I PINNED our mate to the pelts, gripping her hair so she could not look away. "This is the geas talking," I growled. Thorsteinn was right. We were used to an enemy we could see. We kept forgetting that Sorrel was not the one we should be fighting. "The enemy is in your mind, but we will do anything to break the curse. We will not rest until you are healed."

From her prone position, our little fighter blinked up at me, very rapidly. She was holding back tears. Not once had we seen her cry. Not when we took her from the abbey. Not when we ran from the draugr. Not when her leg snapped and exposed the bone. Not when we stood before the Alphas and renounced her as mate.

She would cry now because we had shown her tenderness. A small crack in the wall she put up between us.

"You belong to us, Sorrel," I repeated, shifting my weight off her while still keeping her pinned, "and we will care for you."

"No." She would fight. It was her only answer, when she felt weak. She would learn she didn't have to defend herself from us. She could relax and simply be.

"Yes. This," I grabbed a handful of her tight bottom and squeezed, "is ours. Ours to possess and claim. Ours to punish and to soothe."

"I don't—" her throat worked as if what she would say choked her.

"Tell me," I ordered. We were nose to nose, face to face. She could not move. She had nowhere to run.

"I don't want you to be kind to me," she whispered, breaking my heart.

"It's easier to fight?" I asked and she nodded, face creased in pain.

"Then fight us, Sorrel," I rubbed my chin on the top of her head. "Fight all you want. We will spar with you, and when you are tired, we will hold you until you can fight again."

"You must hate me," she said.

"We do not hate you."

"You do. Everyone does."

"No, little warrior. No."

"You should give me up. Throw me away. I—" she choked now, her eyes squeezing tight. I rolled off her and took her into my arms.

"It's okay to cry," I whispered into her hair. Thorsteinn was beside us now, rubbing her back.

"I can't," she whispered. "I will break apart."

"We will hold you together," Thorsteinn said. "After, we will gather any missing pieces, and return them."

Turning her head, she jammed her fist into her mouth. It could not stop her anguished cry.

"That's it," I murmured as she shook against me. "Cry for me, cry the tears."

It came on her then like a summer gale that blows up quickly and drums fierce rain on the earth. Even at the heart of the storm the sun shone through the clouds.

I held and rocked her, wishing I could pry her heart apart, pick out the sharp rocks that burdened and cut her. I'd put it back together carefully and guard it until it healed.

It did not escape me or Thorsteinn that we were warriors and more comfortable with destruction than the work of holding women when they cried. But this wasn't any woman. This was Sorrel. The beast that ravaged our minds recognized her and laid down its weapons and its rage. In taming her, she tamed us.

Later, much later, I asked, "Feel better?"

She nodded.

I kissed her forehead. Her wet cheeks. Her lips. She sighed and leaned into my kiss.

"Here now," I stripped and settled her on the pelts. "Lie back and let us see to you." The beast within did not fight for control, but the scent and shape of her awakened another, deeper hunger.

"But—"

"No words." I put two fingers at her lips and when she licked at them, I did not try to hide my grin. She felt the same hunger. "That's the way. Let your masters pleasure you. I stroked her flared hips, her tiny waist, the breasts small and firm as new apples. Her muscles rippled under the skin, she trembled. "Shh..."

Thorsteinn lay on the other side of her, touching her, taking liberties. His hands strayed north while mine strayed south. "You are beautiful," he murmured. "Did you know?"

"No," she whispered back. Sweet and compliant. I liked her tough and fighting, I liked her feisty, but soft and open to our touch? She destroyed me.

I knelt between her legs. I kissed her ankle, the inside of her knee until she gasped and pulled away. I grasped her leg more firmly and licked behind her knee until she laughed, a sweet clear sound like a brook in a meadow.

"That's it," Thorsteinn petted her hair, scratching her scalp and kneading her neck.

Her legs fell open and I pounced. My cock ached as I slid hands under her bottom and licked her folds, tasting her honey. She thrashed, her legs kicking over my shoulders and drumming on my back. Thorsteinn grasped her hands and held them over her head, stretching her between us, naked and vulnerable. I crawled over her, marking her with licks and bites and red marks where I fastened my mouth on her and sucked hard. I flipped her over and kissed down her spine, swirled my tongue between her cheeks, nipping her buttocks until she squealed. She writhed against the pelts, her leg cocked so she could rub her mound on one hump. I draped myself over her lower half, rubbing my cock between her cheeks, but did not enter her. This was for Sorrel, only Sorrel. She would forget her sorrow and her pain and remember only opening herself to us and receiving pleasure.

Cock dripping, I dove back between her bottom cheeks, feasting there until she ground frantically against the juice-slicked pelts.

"That's it, rub yourself, take your pleasure," I told her, and thrust my fingers into her sopping hole. As her climax broke, I fucked her gently, withdrawing my fingers only to probe her bottom. She shivered in the aftermath of pleasure. "Good girl," Thorsteinn murmured and bit her ear. "You did well to obey."

She did not even protest. Gleaming with sweat, she slumped onto the pelts. We wrung another climax or two from her sated body, this time with my fingers penetrating the tight circle of her ass.

"Soon we will claim you fully," I told her, and watched in satisfaction as those simple words made her buck and break.

"But not tonight," Thorsteinn said wistfully. We'd spilled our seed on the pelts beside her, surrounding her with our scent.

"Soon," I promised. Sorrel made a small sound, her eyes

heavy and mouth lax. She'd fight us again in the morning. It was in her nature. Any concession of hers was hard won, but worth it.

She gave one last shudder and fell asleep.

Sorrel

The next morning, I lay in bed as long as the warriors let me. Thorsteinn finally approached with a cloth and bucket of water and wiped me down. I squealed at the chilly touch of cloth.

"Should've woken when the water was warm," he chided me. "We would see to you at night, but you fell straight asleep."

I flushed at the memory of so much pleasure.

Vik chuckled knowingly. "Perhaps last night's events will make you more amiable."

"Not likely," I muttered, but lay back and let Thorsteinn caress between my legs with the cloth.

Vik stood and excused himself. "I must ready for today's training," he said and wagged a finger at me before disappearing down the rope ladder. "Be good."

"Good girls get rewards," Thorsteinn promised, before tugging me up. To my dismay, he grasped my collar and guided me to kneel on a pelt near his usual seat.

"You said I could sit on your lap," I whined.

"If I set you on my lap, I will not give you food. I will give you something else." The front of his breeches was tented.

"Perhaps we could..."

He stopped my mouth with his fingers. "We told you we

would claim you when you beg for us. Are you ready to beg?"

I jerked my chin back and forth, pouting.

"Come then. Time to eat." His hand guided me to my knees. "We told you we'd make you our pet. Don't tell me you do not enjoy it." He plucked my nipples, which were hard as pebbles, and awakened a telltale prickle between my legs. I squirmed and refused the first bite. How could I be aroused by this?

"Come, Sorrel. Play the game, pet. Please?" Thorsteinn pressed his forehead against mine. When I nodded his head moved too and I laughed.

He stroked my hair as he fed me.

"I enjoy keeping you naked," he murmured. "If you were truly our pet we would collar and cage you, and keep you undressed. Would you like that?"

I rolled my eyes and accepted more food from his hands.

"Nothing to worry about. Nothing to fear. You just let yourself become ours." He tugged my hair gently, massaging my scalp until I felt half drunk.

"Your nipples stand to attention so prettily." His left hand played with them as he fed me with his right.

Inspired, I curled my tongue around his fingers, lapping up every drop of honey until his eyes turned molten.

"Is that what you like?" he asked, his voice deep and dark.

I nodded. He wanted to play a game? I would win.

Eyes on mine, he scooted back on the stump he used as a seat. He opened his breeches and drew himself out. "There's more for you to lick here, if you like."

Heat flared in my cheeks, arcing through my body. He was changing the rules, but I was caught up in the game.

I scooted forward, accepting the pressure of his hand on

the back of my neck. My tongue flicked at the turgid length. Thorsteinn hummed in pleasure.

"Won't Vik be jealous?"

"If he is jealous, then he's jealous," Thorsteinn said, and tugged my hair so I licked up and down one side of his cock then the other. "Besides, he has taken liberties with you before."

He showed me how to suck him, pinching my nipples to correct me, rolling them gently when I did well. I'd finally learned to take his length several inches into my mouth when he pulled me up. "Here. Straddle my leg." I lay along his heavy thigh, my leaking center set right on his breeches. "You're being such a good girl for me," he crooned. "Rub yourself as you suckle me. Take your pleasure."

I would've whimpered, but he guided my mouth back onto his cock, feeding his length into my mouth inch by inch. His free hand still caressed my breasts, building the fire in me to a raging inferno. Before I knew it, my hips rocked, seeking relief against his hard leg.

"That's it. Obey your master." Reaching down, he spanked my canting bottom. "Faster. Find relief."

Pleasure flicked through me. I danced on its knife edge. The tug on my nipples, the slick patch on Thorsteinn's breeches, the earth and salt taste of him filling my senses— it all combined into a roiling vortex that tossed and shook me.

I moaned around Thorsteinn's cock, and he started spurting, drawing out to bathe my face with his seed. I blinked but met his pleased smile with one of my own.

"Such a good girl," he stroked my hair back from my face. He helped me up and fetched a cloth to clean me. "As much as I love seeing you wear my essence, you can't train with us like this. Too damn distracting."

When he was done, he kissed me thoroughly. At last, reluctantly, he pulled away.

"Come. Vik waits for us."

"What about—" I pointed to the stain I'd left on his clothes.

"If I had time, I'd make you lick it up. We are late, though, so." He shrugged.

"Do you mean," I swallowed. "You will wear them out today?"

"Oh yes, pet." His amusement had a wicked edge. "With pride."

5

S*orrel*

"AFTER YESTERDAY, I thought you would not let me out again," I said as we walked from Yggdrasil.

"You mean after the mist lured you away?" Vik asked. "That was our fault. We should be more vigilant."

"I'm going to scout this area," Thorsteinn grunted. "Stay close to Vik," he ordered me and stalked off, face grim.

My face must have fallen, for Vik put an arm around my shoulders. "He doesn't blame you, Sorrel. He blames himself. If it were up to him, he'd keep you in a stone tower and guard you day and night. He does not like the sneaky tricks of the enemy we fight."

"The spell?" I whispered, as if mentioning it were dangerous.

"Yes. Do not worry, we have plans to break it." He busied himself with laying out the weapons we would use today.

"How?" I wondered. "Is it possible to break such a spell?"

"The mating bond can. It has its own protective magic."

That only filled me with despair. The elusive bond. "And what if it does not form?" I kicked a clod of dirt.

"It will," Vik returned to my side. "Do not worry about that. There is already something between us, can't you feel it?"

I shook my head. He grabbed my hand and pressed it to the bulge in his breeches, laughing when I tugged away.

"That is not bonding," I muttered, flushing.

"Is it not?" Vik's laugh was catching, and I smiled along with him.

"The bond is like water," he said, coming at me slowly, as he would when he taught me to spar. "It flows into any empty spaces." He raised his fist and I blocked the blow. He twisted and I dodged a kick. "And when you least expect it," he feinted left, feinted right, and when I raised my arms to defend myself, he dropped and rolled, coming up beside me and capturing me in his arms. "You're caught," he breathed in my ear.

"Not quite," I raised a foot as he had taught me, and stamped close to his groin, twisting to break his hold. I dropped to the forest floor and he pulled me back by my foot.

"Arr," he growled playfully, "You are quick but not quick enough." He stopped when he saw my face. "What is it?"

"What if it doesn't work? The bonding, breaking the curse, all of it?"

He sobered quickly. "We plan to tell the Alphas we suspect magic is involved. If they understand that, they may be lenient."

Rosalind could have acted under a spell. I could explain

her actions without naming her traitor. We just had to break the spell so I could speak.

"Come on, then," I motioned. "Let's train."

We wrestled under the mild spring sun. Birds flew over our heads, chattering as if they knew the mock battle below them would not end in bloodshed. Vik taught me how to use my body weight to flip a man on his back. Even though I was small, I was fast, and I could use my opponent's height and weight against him and get away.

"Be like a fish," Vik said. "Even if a fisherman catches you, you can thrash and break his grip to slip away."

"You always have me running away."

"If you're faced with a more powerful enemy, yes. Your best weapon is surprise, but after they face you once, you will not surprise them again." He raised his voice, looking beyond me. "Isn't that right, brother?"

"Yes," Thorsteinn straightened from the tree trunk he'd been leaning against. "Listen to my brother, Sorrel. Heed his words."

I rolled my eyes. Not even Thorsteinn's somber mood could dampen my spirits. I pushed a sweaty strand of hair from my face and accepted the drink Vik offered. It occurred to me that I had never been so happy.

"Sorrel's done well. She learns quickly."

"Oh?" Thorsteinn studied me.

I handed the waterskin back to Vik and took a fighting stance. "Come at me."

Setting aside his weapons, he did. I anticipated his feint and ducked his first advance, which came stupidly slow. Thorsteinn faced me again, a hint of surprise on his face.

"She's fast," Vik said from the sidelines, grinning.

"Silence," Thorsteinn grunted. This time he attacked quickly. I got in a blow to his side as I darted away. He followed and seized me, pulling me to face him. "I've seen all your tricks. Got you now."

I darted my head forward as Vik taught me and smashed my skull into his face.

He staggered back

Vik laughed wildly. "The little warrior becomes the master."

I sucked in my breath as Thorsteinn stood with his head tipped back, blood streaming from his nose. "Argh," he growled to the sky, but when he strode back to me, he was laughing. "Well done, little warrior."

"You're not mad at me?"

"For learning the lesson too well?" He ruffled my hair. "Next time we go on patrol, we should take you."

Go on patrol. All happiness left my body. "Did the Alphas give you orders to patrol the far reaches?" I shouldn't ask. I have no right to.

"No," Thorsteinn frowned.

I gnawed my lip. If they left, who would protect me from the pack? I'd be on my own. I'd be safe for a time in the tree lodge, but after a time it would be best to sneak away. Perhaps off the mountain—

"Sorrel," Vik squatted to be at my height, his forehead creasing. "We're not leaving you."

"If the Alphas tell you to, you'll have no choice."

"So eager to be rid of us?" Vik ruffled my hair.

"I only meant, if you had to go, it would be best if I went too—"

Thorsteinn cocked his head, scowling. "Are you so eager to leave?"

I shook my head.

"Come," Thorsteinn's hand clamped onto my arm. He

dragged me a few feet before I got my legs working. His face darkened. I offended him.

"Where are we going?"

"Enough of this play. We have work to do."

I wanted to explain that I had no desire to run from them, but we were walking so fast. I trotted gamely beside him, almost stumbling when he stopped abruptly.

"When we face them, you must remember, I am in charge. You do as I say, immediately. Do you swear?" His grey eyes pierced me, emotions passing over his face like clouds.

"Yes," I blurted, still curious.

"They're there. Over that ridge." He made no move to climb the hill, so I stayed where I was. A strange lowing and shuffling sound made me step closer to him.

The air had a heavy, oppressive weight to it. A scent like an oncoming storm. Even the sun shone dimmer in this place.

"Where are we?"

"At the magical boundary the witches set around the mountain," Vik explained, joining us. His hand ghosted up my back.

"It is not just our patrols that protect you and the spaewives. The Corpse King has ravaged this island to add to his forces. His power grows every moon."

A breeze kicked, scattering dead leaves. I choked on the rotten smell.

"What is that?"

"The Corpse King's forces."

"They're there? Just beyond the hill?" I stared the boulder topped rise with horror. Vik's arms slid around me, and I pressed close.

"It's all right, Sorrel," Thorsteinn said, his voice gentler. He touched my hair. "They cannot get in."

"But how do you leave?"

"You'll see." With one final squeeze, Vik sauntered away. A few steps and he turned. Thorsteinn tossed him something.

"Come," he guided me to follow the tattooed warrior. I held my breath as we grew close to the top of the hill. The stench made my eyes water. I crested the hill and gasped.

The boundary was an invisible line in the brown leaves. On one side, Vik paced, rolling the rune stone between his palm. On the other, an endless line of grey-skinned horrors, dressed in rags. Their rotting faces pressed against the unseen barrier, the bubble of magic that protect the mountain.

"There's so many." I recoiled from the stench, the sight.

"Yes," Thorsteinn agreed grimly. "They are the undead. The Corpse King raises them to do his will." Thorsteinn tugged me back against him and I pressed against him, reassured by his strength.

Vik danced right up to the boundary, tossing the rune stone like a juggler. The undead forces on the other side howled and slavered, bony fingers scrabbling to reach him. He paced back and forth, his powerful body framed by the undead masses. He tossed the rune stone once, twice, catching it lazily.

"What is he doing?" I asked Thorsteinn.

The giant warrior tucked me closer and bid me, "Watch."

Vik found a spot in front of the slavering ranks. He cocked his head... and sent the ball streaking towards the barrier. It blazed a path into the draugr and disappeared. A blast, a boom, a wash of great, bone stripping heat. The earth shook.

Fire flared amid the Corpse King's ranks, flames licking along the rotted clothing, the grey skin and exposed bones. The undead shrieked, opening their mouths with a banshee's scream that died in the roar and crackle of the great fire. Smoke billowed up, blowing over us in a wave of foul ash.

I hid my face against Thorsteinn.

"Balefire," Thorsteinn whispered. "Be brave, little warrior," he murmured.

"It worked." Vik bounded back to our side. I gritted my teeth and faced the boundary again. A hole opened up in the ranks of draugr. Skeletal arms thrashed against the blue sky and were quickly overtaken by the fire. I turned away, pretending the crackling sound was very dry branches in a fire.

"It's new magic," Thorsteinn said, and showed me the rune stones.

Vik took a few more out of his pouch. "Want to try?" He herded me towards the boundary. The hole had filled in, undead snapped their teeth at me. "Pick a spot where they group together."

"Vik," I pressed against him.

"They can't touch you inside the boundary," Vik promised. "The rune stones can reach them. You can do it, little warrior. Remember how they chased us? They took you and your friends."

"Yes," I straightened. "Took us straight to the Corpse King."

"You want to fight," Vik set a rune stone in my hand. "Fight."

I clutched my weapon, weighing it in my hand. Vik pushed my legs apart, correcting my throwing stance. I shut my eyes and remembered the fight after the abbey, after my leg had broken and Vik and Thorsteinn had first tried to make me their mate. The draugr had poured from all directions, overwhelming us. Berserkers dying. Me and my friends taken, terrified. The stone hall of the Corpse King, stinking like a tomb. I took a deep breath, smelled rot.

"Now," Vik ordered, and I threw.

A blast and he shielded me. I peered out between his tattooed forearms at the smoke and destruction I had wrought. And I laughed.

"Another. Give me another."

The rest of the day, I raced up and down the boundary line. The draugr poured into each opening, their ranks endless as a vast, stinking ocean. At times, Thorsteinn and Vik would wade into the fray, crossing the boundary and sending draugr flying to their doom.

We fell into a rhythm. I would throw my rune stone, they would follow, roaring, to scythe down any foe that remained standing. When the ranks of draugr replenished and overwhelmed them, they retreated long enough for me to throw again.

"Will it ever end?" I coughed on some leftover smoke.

"Tired?" Vik offered me a water skin. His skin was slick with sweat and the fluids of the dying draugr. His chest heaved and he had cuts on his arms from the enemy's weapons. As I drank, the worst of them healed before my eyes. Vik's grin was bigger than I'd ever seen.

"No," I shoved the container back at him and took out my sling. "Let's go again!"

Bit by bit, blast by blast, we cut down the enemy. At last I could tell—when the draugr rushed to replenish their line against the boundary, the ranks had thinned. They didn't stretch as far as the eye could see.

"It's working," I shouted. "We're winning!"

Vik banged on his shield, snarling happily at the enemy. Thorsteinn was calmer, waiting for the blast with his axe and spear outstretched. He fought with no shield. Vik didn't hide behind his, but sent it crashing through the dead men's ranks, mowing down several at a time.

I strode to the boundary edge, pacing fearlessly in front of it. The draugr had learn to recoil from the sight of the rune stone, but when I hid it in the sling, they pressed against the boundary again, slavering as they tried to reach me. I swung my sling, waiting for more to gather in one spot so I could destroy them. We would clear the enemy out of this side of the mountain. And I would've helped.

I sent the ball flying deep into the knot of undead. Balefire blew right in the center of their ranks. I stood firm and faced it, my face singed with the heat but nothing else. Dust and limbs rained down on the draugr as Thorsteinn and Vik swooped in, closing in on either end and hacking down the enemy until they met in the middle and faced out again to pick off any standing undead.

"Almost done, little warrior," Vik shouted.

And then I saw it. High above the fray, in a dark cloud, seething with fog and flashes of lightning, the shape of a tall skeleton. It couldn't be real. The Corpse King couldn't be here. But he'd appeared this way before, and each time, it was real enough.

"No," I shrieked. Loading my sling, I threw. The rune stone exploded above the warrior's heads—they dove for cover. But the balefire did not touch the dark figure.

I stumbled backwards and was swallowed by a patch of mist. And then I was not safe on my side of the boundaries. The draugr's scent surrounded me. Draugr, every-where. Grey faces pressing on me, bony fingers dragging me.

I cried out and kicked backwards, fumbling with a rune stone. It slipped from my fingers—

"Sorrel, no!" Vik dove and landed before me, catching the fallen rune stone. As soon as he caught it, he sent it streaking into the draugr's ranks. Another boom and a stinking veil of charred bone covered my face and suffocated me.

"The Corpse King," I screamed, and choked. Thorsteinn was shouting something.

Vik grabbed me and, bent double, racing from the boundary. I kept my head down, burrowing against Vik's chest to find the leather and fur smell of him instead.

Finally, we were clear. The sun shone around us, and there was no boundary, no mist, no Corpse King apparition hovering in the air. Just a clear sky and clean air. I sucked in lungfuls, collapsed against Vik.

He held a cup to my lips, and I drank long, greedy draughts of the cold water. "Are you all right?"

"Better." I gasped while he filled another cup.

"More," he ordered, and I drank again. He wiped my face with a cool cloth.

"Forgive me," I said. "I thought... I thought I saw the Corpse King. There was mist, and it surrounded me. It took me somewhere."

"We saw. There was mist, Sorrel, but you were still with us. You ran across the boundary."

I shook my head, exhausted. "I was confused. The last time the Corpse King appeared..." *Rosalind nearly died.*

"You were captured," Vik finished for me. He knew about the first time. Not the second.

"We remember," Thorsteinn said, his voice taut. "We never would've taken you to that place if we knew..."

"How it would affect me?" I scrubbed my face. "You couldn't know. I didn't."

"You were taken with your friends," Vik continued, "but you never wanted to speak of it before."

"I didn't like remembering. I didn't let myself remember." It had blurred away like a bad dream.

"It might help to speak of it," Thorsteinn said.

I nodded. So many memories I'd locked up, but it'd done nothing to help me.

Vik rubbed my back. "Are you ready to tell us what happened?"

I squeezed my eyes shut. I couldn't share what happened that fateful day with Rosalind, but I could tell them what happened last fall. It was so long ago.

"We came upon the Berserkers fighting the draugr. You left me in the tree," my voice wavered. "And ran into the fray."

"We thought you'd be safe there," Vik murmured.

"I was," I covered my face with my hands. I had never told them this. "I would've been... if I hadn't left."

"What?" Thorsteinn's growl ripped into me.

"It was my fault I was taken. I heard my friends screaming... and I couldn't stay safe while they were taken."

Silence. My warriors were angry with me. I might as well tell the rest.

"I ran to save them. I did not know what I would do. But after the mating bite, I felt stronger. Fast. Powerful."

"The bond at work," Vik muttered.

"I did not think I could save them, but I had to do what I could. I had my sling. I came upon one draugr and beat it back." I hadn't known what I faced. The mist was swirling thick, I only knew I was living a nightmare. "I reached my friends in time for him to appear." I shuddered. "And then we were someplace else." I shook my head. I knew what I described was impossible. "I woke up laying in a stone hall. My friends lay around me, asleep. Almost all of them." One had been awake, her golden head shining in the gloom. Rosalind. "There was a... figure... in the darkness. Tall, taller than any man. Dressed in robes, but so thin." My voice dropped to a whisper. "He was barely a skeleton. A corpse."

"The Corpse King," Vik growled, and I startled, remembering what I was telling them. "He was speaking to Rosalind. His hands reached out to touch her head and I-I had to do something. I still had my sling."

"You attacked the Corpse King?"

"I d-didn't mean to," I stuttered. "I wasn't thinking. I knew he would hurt her. I just knew. I flung a rock at his head. I ran forward and grabbed Rosalind. Suddenly we were outside, back in the forest. All of us. We roused the others and kept moving. You found us again."

"You saved them. Your sister orphans."

"I just did what I had to do."

"Does Rosalind remember this?"

"I think so. She hates me though." How else could I explain her coldness, her stinging remarks?

Thorsteinn and Vik exchanged glances.

"Sorrel, when... if Rosalind wakes, will her story damn you?"

I shut my eyes. "Yes," I whispered. I had used my sling again. I had shot her. "Forgive me. I didn't know what else to do."

"You shot her for a reason. Just as you shot the Corpse King when you were taken on the journey from the abbey to our mountain."

"Yes." I let my head fall back with a thunk and a hand passed over my brow.

"Rest now, little warrior. You're safe here. We will take care of everything."

~

THE DREAM PLAYED in my head with the confidence of reality. Rosalind's bright head glowed against the shadowy figure who loomed over her. Skeletal hands reached down. I swung my sling and let the stone fly. But unlike the first time I shot the Corpse King, the missile did not harm him. It disappeared into the mist, and the menacing figure continued reaching for my friend.

The moonstone, Rosalind had told me. We must fetch it before he does. If he gets it, all is lost, for it feeds his power. And here she was, faced with the Corpse King, offering up the glowing stone.

I did not hesitate. Feeding another stone into my sling, I swung hard and fast—and hit my target—Rosalind's golden head. She dropped to the ground. The shadow of the Corpse King hovered over her, hissing. I raced to claim the moonstone—and ran into a thick mist. The fog swallowed me whole. I could not see my arms in front of my face. My foot hit an obstacle and I stumbled and came face to face with Rosalind's still features. She lay on the forest floor, blood leaking from her skull. The moonstone was gone. So was the Corpse King.

A squawk above my head had me searching the trees. A black bird sat on a branch above our heads and in its beak the moonstone gleamed.

"Give it back," I said, rising with sling in hand. I did not have another stone. "Please. We must keep it safe."

The raven ruffled its wings and disappeared. I stared at the empty branch. It wavered a little as if a bird had just launched from it, and for that, I was grateful. Otherwise I'd know I'd gone mad.

At my feet, Rosalind bled into the dirt. She'd led me all this way, tricking me into helping her find the moonstone, only to offer it to our enemy in the end. Did the Corpse King own her mind? Was she tricked?

Before I could drop to my knees and bind her head, a shout made me raise my empty sling. That was how the Berserkers found me, useless weapon upraised, my fellow orphan and spaewife unconscious at my feet.

They bound me and brought me back to the mountain. I tried to explain about the Corpse King, moonstone, and raven, but they thought it nonsense. I did not tell them what Rosalind had done. How could I name her traitor when she had no voice to defend herself?

"Sorrel," someone called across a great distance. "Sorrel, come back to us." Thorsteinn and Vik. But they couldn't want me. Even if they did, there was another figure striding towards me out of the mist, bony hands outstretched to take me—

"The Corpse King," I thrashed. "He is coming."

"He's not here," Thorsteinn's deep voice intoned. His fingers smoothed my cheeks. "We're here."

I opened my eyes. "You left me." I lay in the dark tree lodge, two warriors outstretched on either side of me.

On my left Vik cleared his throat. "We left because we are cursed. Without a mate we will go mad."

"I thought I was your mate."

"We tried," Thorsteinn said. "We claimed you. But after you were taken by the Corpse King the bond was broken, and nothing we did could revive it. You were closed to us and in time, we thought you would choose another."

"It was easier to accept patrols on the far side of the island, than to stay here and try to make you love us. If you did not want us, we would go mad," Vik smoothed my hair from my face and bent his until our foreheads touched.

"Forgive us, Sorrel. We did wrong. I had a woman, long ago. Hildr was a shield maiden, a woman warrior, like you," Thorsteinn said. "She and I disagreed right before we went into battle. I wanted her to stay safe; she wanted to fight. In battle, I told her to wait for my signal. She disobeyed and ran into the enemy's ranks herself. They cut her down before I could reach her."

I put my hand to Thorsteinn's cheek, and he leaned into it. "I lost my first love because I could not make her obey. And Vik's mother left him and his father over and over."

"We could not make her stay," Vik murmured. "Sometimes it is easier to leave before your loved one leaves you."

"And now," I rasped. Vik reached behind him and handed me a cup. I drank and repeated. "Now, what will you do with me?"

"We're not leaving. We're never leaving you again. We swear it."

I lay back down between them. My hand slipped to Vik and found his hand. Thorsteinn clasped the other. Perhaps we would never be mates, but we would be together.

∾

I WOKE BETWEEN THE WARRIORS. A heavy pelt covered my body. I slung it off. I was hot, too hot, with sweat trickling down my back.

At my side Vik muttered something. He rolled and his arm flopped around me. Another mumble, and he pulled me close.

I wriggled around in his arms. His eyes were shut, dark lashes fanned over his tattooed cheeks. His nose was crooked at the top. His mouth, perfectly formed. I craned my neck and touched my lips to his.

His eyes opened.

"Thorsteinn," he growled. "Wake."

"What?" Thorsteinn grunted.

"Sorrel. She's in heat."

I arched my body, tugging at my jerkin. The leather was too heavy, too rough for my body. I writhed, trying to get free.

"Easy, easy," Thorsteinn murmured at my back.

"I have to... I need..." I was almost crying, tearing at my collar. Vik rose up and helped me strip out of my clothes, a snake shedding its skin. Cool air hit my body, but it wasn't enough. I kicked out of my breeches and lay back, panting.

"Shhh," Thorsteinn hushed me. His hand lifted the hair from the back of my neck and pressed a kiss there. The tender touch shot through me like lightning, illuminating the storm. My hips rocked, I rolled and threw myself at him.

"Sorrel," he mouthed, his lips moving under mine. I grabbed his braid and jerked him closer, mashing my mouth against his.

"Sorrel," he was laughing. I rubbed my breasts against the coarse hair on his chest, arching like a cat, purring with pleasure at the perfect abrasion.

Fist in my hair, he tugged me back. "You're in heat."

Rolling my hips against his, I nodded. I had experienced this once before, at the abbey. I had hidden myself away and suffered. This time, I would not have to hide or suffer.

Vik cursed.

"You want this?" Thorsteinn snapped his hips upward. His hardness met the needy space between my legs and my eyes rolled back in my head. I shivered and moaned.

"Tell me," he ordered, still gripping my hair, keeping me from moving the way I wanted. "Beg for my cock."

"I want," I licked my lips.

He ground his cock against me. "Say it."

"I want you," I hissed, digging my fingers in his shoulders, panicked that he might pull away. "I need this."

"This?" His left hand tugged my hair as his right fished in his breeches, drawing out his perfect length. "You need my cock?"

"Yes."

Vik was behind me, his hands spanning my waist lifting and holding me aloft long enough for Thorsteinn to guide himself inside me.

I exhaled happiness, kneading the muscles on Thorsteinn's chest. "Ah, yes. Yes." Lightning sizzled along my spine, awakening every inch of my body. I felt Thorsteinn from the tips of my toes to the top of my skull. My nipples hardened to points.

"Show me," Thorsteinn commanded. "Show me how much you need me."

I rocked forward,

"That's it, little one. That's the way." He took my hips and steadied me. Vik stood beside us, gripping his own cock, his eyes hooded.

"Hold tight," Thorsteinn said. "I will give you what you need." His body hardened under my scrabbling fingers, his arms turning to granite as he slammed his cock into me from below. I howled and would've fallen if Thorsteinn hadn't dug his fingers into my buttocks.

Vik took hold of my hair. "Suck me," he directed his cock into my willing mouth. I tongued down his length, looking up for approval.

"Yes, that's the way," Vik crooned even as his hand guided me.

"This is the beginning," Thorsteinn whispered as his fingers stroked my sides. My body tingled with his promise. "This is our claim. You belong to us, and no other."

"Yes," I cried as heat rolled through me, pleasure singing in its wake. My muscles tightened and my body bowed, thrumming with sensation.

"Again," Thorsteinn said, and pulled my hips into his.

They claimed me over and over, mounting me again and again while I cried out for release. At last Thorsteinn pulled me atop his body and I rode him, too weary to speak, my body clenching around him until lightning flashed up my spine and I collapsed, and he had to roll me to the side and finish that way.

Outside the birds sung a new day.

THE SUN WAS high when the warriors and I finally left the lodge.

"Shall we spar today?" I asked, snacking on an apple. Even after a full breakfast, I was still hungry.

"Spar?" Thorsteinn ruffled my hair. "Is that what you wish? I thought we wrestled enough last night."

I flushed and Vik stole my apple, biting into it with a wink.

"Sorrel," Thorsteinn's hand caught my shoulder, pulling me back just before I heard a shout. A warrior strode down the hill towards our tree home.

"Knut," Vik straightened and greeted him. I hung back, even as Thorsteinn squeezed my shoulder reassuringly. I knew I shouldn't look at the warrior directly, but something in the visitor's face set warning bells inside me clanging, and I couldn't look away.

"How goes it this morning?" Thorsteinn called.

"Thorsteinn, Vik," Knut greeted us in a deep voice. He looked at me. I shrank behind Thorsteinn. "Have you completed your bond?"

Thorsteinn's hand flexed on my shoulder. "Why? Do the Alphas wish to test us? It hasn't been a moon."

"You've run out of time." Knut looked from one warrior to the other. "Rosalind has woken up."

6

S *orrel*

THE WARRIORS BUNDLED me in a cloak smelling of them, walked me quickly to a side of the mountain I'd never been before.

"I'll leave you here," Knut said as we came to the mouth of a cave. "The Alphas are waiting."

"Come," Thorsteinn pushed me towards the dark entrance. I shrank back, my legs turning to stone.

"Shhh, it's all right. See?" Vik bounded inside. "It's not a dead end. It's a secret entrance into the mountain."

"What are we doing here?" I asked now that Knut was gone. The past minutes, my stomach had sloshed, threatening to expel everything I'd eaten. I clung to the warriors until my knuckles were white.

"The Alphas will summon us to check our bond." Thorsteinn said and motioned me inside. "Here," he said to

Vik, who'd found a torch by the entrance and lit it. "This is as good a place as any."

"What are you doing?" I asked when they lifted me onto a rock and faced me. The light of the torch surrounded us with flickering shadow. Outside the small sphere of light—darkness. I swallowed.

"Sorrel, do you remember when we said the bond could break a spell?" Vik asked.

"Yes."

"It's time to try." Thorsteinn said, leaning close. *Open yourself, little one. Do not be afraid.* I startled as his voice echoed in my mind.

"It's all right," Vik gathered my hands in his. "This is the way."

"I can't—" Where there once was a barrier, a door blocking the way, there was nothing. But there was no light either. Only darkness, and I recoiled from it. "I can't do this."

You can, Thorsteinn said from just beyond the door. The darkness shrank and he stepped through.

Show me what happened. Don't speak. Show me.

Vik's hands tightened on mine. "Close your eyes, Sorrel." I stared at him and a smile quirked the corner of his mouth. "For once, do as you're told."

Thorsteinn smiled. The flame flickered over his faces, but there was no anger or blame there.

I could do this.

I closed my eyes—

Midnight. The moon was a sliver of light reflecting off left-over patches of snow when Rosalind left the lodge. Moonlight glinting off her bright hair as I followed her. It wasn't like her to leave.

"Sorrel?" Juliet was outside, huddled in the shadows. She hid out there often because she went into heat. A former nun, she

was terrified the Berserkers would find out, and force her to mate.

"Did Rosalind come this way?" I asked.

Juliet nodded her face pained. "I should go after her. She's been acting strangely lately." Juliet didn't have to explain. Rosalind had been quieter than usual. At night, she tossed and turned with bad dreams. During the day, no one was spared her sharp tongue, not even her beloved sister Aspen.

"I'll do it. I'll see what she's up to." I brushed Juliet's shoulder as I passed.

"Bring her back," the former nun called after me.

It made no sense, I thought as I tracked Rosalind through the trees. She wore a cloak but didn't bother to cover her bright head. The moon turned her blonde hair to silver. Why would she leave now? She'd mocked me about my plans to live in the wilderness, but her teasing had a jealous edge. She made no secret of her dislike of the Berserkers and her desire to escape, but I never thought she would act. The Rosalind I knew would never leave her sister behind.

Fog lay across our path. I hurried through the milky mist, trying and failing to catch up with Rosalind. Through the trees, firelight flickered, and men's voices rose, rough and deep. Our guards enjoying their midnight watch. I slunk in the shadows, hiding behind trees. Rosalind did nothing to hide herself, but still, no warrior looked up or took note. And so, we made our escape off the mountain.

All night we walked, and I kept waiting for Rosalind to hear me and turn. The night was still. No Berserker patrols, no howling wolves, not even a hooting owl. The further we hiked away from the mountain, the more my dread grew. Any minute we might come upon a host of draugr and be captured, but whenever I tried to catch up to Rosalind to warn her, I never could.

It went on for hours, like a dream. The mist grew thick

between us. I knew if I didn't catch up to her now, I never would. So, I ran. And eventually, I caught her.

"Rosalind?" Her eyes were glassy, vacant as a deep pool. Could she be sleep walking? I shook her, but she never woke. Her gaze fixed on some spot in the distance, she marched onward.

Nothing I said or did made her stop walking. She seemed almost asleep—until first light. Dawn struck her face, and she came awake. "Sorrel," she greeted me. "You're here. We must find the moonstone."

"What moonstone?"

"I had a dream of a stone of great power. The Corpse King sought it long ago. It was formed by the magic of the spaewives, the women he took to wife. In his hands it could increase his power, make him unstoppable. But we can stop him, if we find the stone. In the right hands, it can bind him for a thousand years."

"And you know where to find it?"

"This way," she said, and hurried on. I did not like it, but I followed. Rosalind was with me when we were captured by the Corpse King. He had spoken to her. Perhaps that is how she knew of the moonstone.

I didn't realize she was in league with him, until too late.

We walked for another day, maybe a night and a day. The mist surrounded us, and time blurred together. I thought it strange there were no draugr. But perhaps Rosalind was right— she'd had a dream, a vision, and her journey was blessed by the Goddess.

I know now that the Corpse King led her on by the mist and kept his own forces away.

We came to a stream. We followed it until I heard the roar of the waterfall.

"Here. The moonstone is here," Rosalind said. We walked the mossy bank of the pool, overturning clumps of dead leaves. I kicked over a rock and it rolled, breaking through a screen of leaves and branches of a fallen tree. And there it was: a hint of milky light at the bottom of a great pit.

"Look," I got to my belly and peered into the pit, deep enough to cover three men standing on each other's shoulders. The moonstone shone at the bottom. It was the size of my hand and the glow drew the eye...

"You'll have to climb down," Rosalind said. "And fetch it."

"Why me?"

She motioned to the breeches I always wore.

With a sigh, I got a long branch and tried to fish for the stone. The pit was too deep for that, but Rosalind was right. I could climb down. I just didn't want to. I couldn't stand the darkness, or the feeling of being closed in.

But the light drew me. Rolling up my breeches, I took the branch and used it to aid my way down. The moonstone pulsed brighter as I grew close. For a moment I thought I heard a chorus of women's voices whispering in my ear—

"Lift it up," Rosalind ordered. I was reluctant to release it, but it would be easier to climb without the stone in my hands. It was heavier than I'd imagined, set in silver, with the remnants of a chain. I snagged the chain with a branch and lifted it up to Rosalind. As soon as she grabbed it, she drew back from the pit.

"Help me up," I called. "Rosalind?"

But she was gone. The walls of the pit closed in. It was like the torture I endured back at the abbey, trapped in a dark space. My palm still tingled where the moonstone had touched it. Closing my eyes, I found new strength to climb up.

When I reached the top, the mist was so thick, I could no longer see the waterfall.

"Rosalind?" I called. Her footsteps led away from the pit. The leaves were turned in such a way, I knew from my lessons in tracking she was in a hurry.

I fought my way through the mist, which seemed as thick as

water. I was not surprised when I came upon Rosalind gazing up at a tall cloaked figure. I'd seen her in such a position before, when we were first captured by the Corpse King.

Only this time she held the moonstone. In his hands it could increase his power, make him unstoppable.

My hand was on my sling before I could think. I had one shot. After that, the Corpse King would know I was there. I loaded and wound up the sling and aimed for Rosalind.

As soon as the stone struck her temple, she fell. The moonstone hit the ground. I ran forward. There was a flash of light, like balefire, and the tall apparition disappeared.

Before I could reach it, a raven swooped down and grabbed the moonstone, and flew up to a tree branch. The raven also disappeared.

The mist swirled away, and I was surrounded by Berserkers. Rosalind lay there with blood on her head. I had a sling in my hand. The warriors knew what happened. They pounced on me and tied me up. They told me I'd be put to death. I told them I didn't want to hurt her, but they didn't believe me. I was guilty. Guilty...

"Sorrel." A hand cupped my chin. I startled at its warmth. Thorsteinn looked down at me, sober face creased with intent. "Are you with us?"

"Yes," I said, and even though I felt sick from remembering, but I felt lighter.

"Good girl," he murmured, drawing me into his embrace. His arms went around me, and he tucked a pelt around my shoulders. "You did well."

I shivered, and Vik came closer with the torch. The light danced around us, illuminating the large passage. As caves go, this one was spacious and dry. Someone kept it clean of cobwebs.

"You saw it then?" I asked. "All of it?"

"We did."

"You're... you're not mad at me?"

Thorsteinn drew back. "For what?'

"For all of it. Leaving the mountain. Hurting Rosalind. I had to stop her. She would give away the stone, and all would be lost. Either she was tricked, or she'd sided with the enemy when we first were captured."

"We know." he rubbed his stubbled chin against my cheek. "You did nothing wrong. We know that now."

"We should have trusted you from the first," Vik muttered. "Sorrel, we failed you."

"We must tell the Alphas everything. If the Corpse King has the moonstone—"

"What about Rosalind," I interrupted. "Will she be in trouble?"

"If she did in fact betray us, we must be prepared. She might tell more lies and bring doom upon the whole mountain," Thorsteinn explained.

I sagged against him. "I don't want to name her traitor. I know how the Corpse King can trick a mind."

"So do the Alphas. They will consider this when they hear of her crimes."

"What is this moonstone, and can it do what Rosalind claims?" Vik stroked his beard.

"I've heard stories of the witch using a stone to bind the King long ago," Thorsteinn said. "But it has not been found. If this is the same stone Rosalind sought, we may have a way to defeat our enemy."

"Let's tell the Alphas," Vik said, and gestured for Thorsteinn and me to precede him through the tunnel.

I held my breath as we walked through the flickering shadows, but even after many paces the air moved cool and sweet against my face. We were not going to run out of air. I relaxed.

At last we came to a dimly lit chamber furnished with a rug and several chairs. Braziers lined the room, their fire casting warmth and light.

"Who made this place?" I asked.

"This? This is one of the Alphas' anterooms," Thorsteinn shrugged. "The head Alpha, Samuel, fashions it after the histories he reads."

I blinked at this, and Vik set down the torch and shoved Thorsteinn. "She means the tunnels. Who carved out the mountain."

"Oh," Thorsteinn frowned, glancing around the room. "Dwarves, probably. Long ago."

I didn't know such creatures existed, but before I could ask more, a warrior strode into the room.

"Thorsteinn, Vik," he greeted my warriors. Both bowed their heads slightly in respect, telling me this tall visitor was an Alpha. I peered around Vik, trying to place him. I recognized him from my trial at the standing rocks before Thorsteinn shifted his weight and blocked my view. He and Vik stood squarely between me and the Alpha, their stance respectful but clear: if anyone tried to grab me, they would fight.

"How goes it," the Alpha asked.

"Well. Sorrel has been obedient. The perfect mate," Thorsteinn said with such certainty, I almost believed him.

I hid my face behind his broad back before I could betray the truth. Vik reached back to clamp a hand on my shoulder, silencing me.

"You've no reason to punish her?" The Alpha's solemn voice tempered with a slight spark of something as he surveyed the three of us. Amusement at Thorsteinn and Vik's protectiveness, perhaps.

"Do we need a reason to discipline our mate?" Vik asked, a sliver of humor in his tone to match the Alpha's. "Sorrel has the sense to submit when she is bested. The struggle to bend her to our will is pure pleasure."

I started blushing.

The Alpha cleared his throat. "I see," he ran a hand over his blond beard, a gesture Vik did often when he wanted to hide a smile. "So, the bond has formed?"

"We have reason to believe so, yes."

"Will it survive a test?" The Alpha continued gravely.

Thorsteinn hesitated. My body went into freefall, tumbling from a great height for every silent second. "In time," the grey-eyed warrior said finally. "We were given a moon."

"Yes, but things change." The Alpha motioned, and slowly, reluctantly, Vik drew me out from behind Thorsteinn and set me before him. His hands rested on my shoulder, I put my own hands up to grip his.

"Rosalind's awake," the Alpha addressed me. "She came to last night but was in great pain. The healer gave her a sleeping draught to help the ache in her head, but we believe Rosalind will wake again any moment, and be able to speak clearly."

"We called you here, Sorrel, to give you another chance tell your side of the story. The pack is calling for your death," the Alpha reminded me when I pressed my lips together.

"We know what happened," Thorsteinn said. "None of it was Sorrel's fault. In fact, she may have saved us all." Taking a deep breath, Thorsteinn repeated everything I had shown him. Vik gathered me in his arms, and I leaned against his body.

"Is this true?" The Alpha asked when Thorsteinn had finished. I nodded. The Alpha frowned. "This is grave indeed to realize it's possible for the Corpse King to stretch out his hand and bespell our spaewives, breaching the protections we have set around the mountain—"

"Sorrel and Rosalind were captured. Early on, before they came to the mountain. The spell could've taken root there. The Corpse King may have cursed Sorrel so she could not speak of his presence. And he may have bespelled Rosalind even further."

"There are many questions to answer," The Alpha tugged his beard. "Where is this moonstone? Why would the raven take it? We will send word to the witch who first told us of the moonstone. She will give us more insight. There is much to learn."

"If Sorrel is right, and Rosalind betrayed the pack, then Sorrel's actions saved us all," Thorsteinn said shortly.

"Yes, yes," the Alpha murmured. "Well done, little warrior," he said to me. To Thorsteinn and Vik he said, "Take your mate, and continue to work on the bond. "But take a care. There are many who resent that she is walking around free. See that she stays far away from them, on your side of the mountain."

Vik

OUR LITTLE WARRIOR brooded all the way back to the tree lodge. I don't think she noticed that we took a different route, going the far way around the more populated parts of the mountain. We stayed close to the boundary, going far closer than any other warrior would with their mate. But what we told the Alpha Ragnvald was right: Sorrel is no ordinary mate. She is strong within and without. She was born to put up a fight.

Just as we were born to subdue and protect her. The push and pull between us challenges and soothes the beast. With Sorrel, life won't ever be calm. We wouldn't want it any other way.

I started laughing as I realized it. Sorrel shot me a disgusted look.

"I'm glad you're happy," she muttered.

"You're here, we're here, and free," I swept my hand around the empty path. "The day is fine. Why shouldn't I be?"

"Because my friend lies with her head broken—because I broke it," she hissed. "Because the pack wants me dead. Because I was cursed—" She kept murmuring angrily even as I stopped her mouth with mine. I kissed her until she sunk her teeth in to my lip and drew blood. And then I laughed again.

"I can't believe... oh..." she snarled, and ran at me, ducking at the last to strike my body the way I taught her. I twisted and caught her—I showed her the battle move, after all—and threw her over my shoulder.

"Race you," I mouthed to Thorsteinn, who still looked grim. "And you," I swatted Sorrel's backside, "Be quiet. We don't want to draw attention, do we?"

She wriggled and fought all the way back to the lodge, stilling only long enough for me to climb up into our home. She went so quiet, I knew she was planning something.

Sure enough, once my feet touched the sturdy floorboards, she writhed and slipped away, quick as a fish. She grabbed my knife and came at me, ready to stab me. "My little wolf, armed with one sharp tooth. Do you wish to see me bleed? Do your worst."

I faced her, and she came at me, again and again. I matched her movements, blocking blows, feinting the opposite way.

In the end she was breathing hard.

"Finished?" I asked.

She nodded.

I wiped the blood off my arm where I let my guard down and she cut me. The gleam of victory in her eyes is worth it. I stripped off my jerkin and was rewarded with a heated rush of scent. "Ready to fuck?"

Eyes locked on my naked torso, she nodded.

"Finally," Thorsteinn muttered, entering the lodge.

"Our mate is ready, but not subdued," I told him. "I think it's time we showed her what we do with mates who will not submit."

Thorsteinn clamped an arm around Sorrel and drew her back against him.

"I made something for you," I told her, and unleashed a rope to lower a sturdy frame made of lashed branches.

Her face goes blank. "A cage? You got me a cage?"

"You will like this one," Thorsteinn promised. Still, it was a fight to get her inside. Between the two of us, we got her naked and trapped inside. She ended up on all fours, still able to contort and move.

"That will not work," I murmured, so we caught her wrists and lashed them to the bottom rungs as she spat and tried to gnaw at us. Once her front was secure, I tied her legs apart, so her haunches splayed to either corner of the cage, her holes perfectly on display.

"It works," I said.

Thorsteinn grunted.

"Let me out," Sorrel tugged her bonds.

"No. Not until you please us." My breeches were uncomfortably tight, so I undid them.

"Put that cock near me and I'll bite it off," Sorrel snarled.

"Then you will be in there a long time." Thorsteinn rapped the cage frame.

She bared her teeth.

I turned away. "What say you, Thorsteinn, shall we have a fire? Or go for a hunt? There's another boar we could—"

"All right," Sorrel muttered. "Fine."

I'd made the bars wide enough for us to reach our hands through. We did that now, stroking her back and legs.

I grinned at her. "I told you you would like this cage."

"Well, I don't. I don't like it at all."

"Because you don't know how to enjoy it."

She glared.

"Close your eyes." I waited until she did and rewarded her by running my hand down her back. Thorsteinn joined me on the other side, and together we rubbed down our mate, massaging her tight neck and shoulders, squeezing her legs and patting her backside and haunches.

"There," he murmured, squatting to inspect her nether lips. "I knew you'd enjoy it."

Sure enough, the skin between her thighs shone with arousal. There was a large enough gap in the bars for Thorsteinn to reach in and tease the plump lips. Sorrel gasped and tried to get away at first, but Thorsteinn pressed his face against the bars, angling his head just right for him to lick the tender juncture.

I reached in and squeezed her small breasts, tugging the nipples and enjoying the way her back arched to follow my touch.

After long minutes, her breathing grew more ragged. Her head dropped. I went around tugged her face up by her hair and met her lips.

"I don't—" she started, and I kissed the protest away.

"Calm. You cannot move, remember? You cannot get out until we allow it. You can only... be."

"Be what?" she asks her voice slurred. Drunk on sensation.

"Be ours, little warrior," I whispered. I fed her my fingers, she took them in her mouth, sucking. My cock throbbed, swelling and threatening to split my breeches. I freed it and it curled up against my belly, leaking.

Thorsteinn kept licking her, taking advantage of her helpless state. He gripped her bottom, alternately squeezing and smacking it. She arched her back, pressing her backside against the cage, mewling. He dipped his fingers into her. She stiffened and trembled, her mouth slackening. My fingers pushed back her moan. Her tongue curled around the rough digits, licking as I fucked her mouth with my hand.

"That's it," I growled. A slight quiver went through her body. The cage creaked as she rocked on Thorsteinn's fingers, moving as much as the tight bonds would allow. As I reached my free hand in and plucked her peaked nipples, she moaned again. Her climax rippled through her. The cage shook.

I could stand it no longer. I stepped away long enough to take the rope and unwind it from the hook, lowering the cage so it settled between Thorsteinn and me. Sorrel craned her neck to look up at me. Her face was now the right height to suck my cock.

"Gently. No teeth. Bite us and you will live in here," I rapped the cage. "Understand?"

Her answer was garbled as her mouth was filled. I hissed as she took me deep. Her tongue licked along my veined length, finding every sensitive spot. My balls hung heavy, filled with all the cum in the world, ready to erupt into her perfect mouth. I gripped her hair and tugged this way and that, teaching her exactly how to please me.

Across from me, Thorsteinn dropped his breeches. Sorrel hummed around my cock as he breached her pussy. The cage swayed between us. Every time he thrust, she took my cock deeper. Steadying the cage with both hands, I pushed her back. We worked into a rhythm, moving her back and forth between us. Her hands clenched against the bars, her nipples hardened and her eyes fluttering closed as we filled her. Best of all, she could not move or speak. We'd taken away all choices, and the only one left was to let us use her for our pleasure and her own.

Thorsteinn must have reached between her legs to stimulate her again, because she shook with another climax, gasping around my cock. I thrust deep into her throat and shot my cum into her gullet. She choked a little, tears leaking from her eyes, but she took all I had to give. I cradled her face as I drew out and wiped the tears from her cheeks.

"Well done, little one," I praised her, kissing her. She smiled against my lips.

"You're a braver man than I," Thorsteinn muttered. I stepped back and let him finish. Sorrel cried out as he thrust in and out, gripping the cage tight and slamming into her. The lodge filled with the slap of skin on wet skin. Sorrel writhed and shuddered, climaxes overtaking her again and again. With a roar, Thorsteinn came.

I waited a mere minute before undoing her bonds and letting her slump down with a contented sigh.

"See?" I told her smugly. "I told you you would like the cage."

7

S *orrel*

"Sorrel," Vik shook me awake. "Sorrel, wake up."

"What is it?" I met the grim faces of the warriors.

"The Alphas have summoned us. We must go, but you are staying here."

I rubbed my face. My body was sore but sated from our antics with the cage. It was still night, though. A few birds sang in the darkness.

Outside, someone called for Thorsteinn. I shrank back in the pelts.

"What is happening? Who is that?"

"The Alphas have called the pack to gather at the standing stones. We go to tell your story but leave you with a guard."

"Why can't I go with you?"

"Too dangerous. There are some warriors who are

enraged over the events. The Alphas want to speak to the pack without distraction."

And I was a distraction. I swallowed. "I don't want you to leave me."

"We aren't leaving for long. Just for a time. We'll come back to you, Sorrel, we swear it." I let Vik crush me to him, closing my eyes as he kissed my hair.

"Draw the rope ladder up after us," Thorsteinn ordered before they left.

I watched them climb down and greet the warrior who was to be my guard. Knut, I remembered. Hazel's mate.

"Sorrel," Thorsteinn tugged the rope ladder, and waited until I drew it back up to lope down the path that would take them to the standing stones. Knut took his place beside the tree, half in, half out of shadows.

I sat by the low fire and tried to focus on sharpening my arrowheads but could not settle. What if the Alphas did not believe Thorsteinn and Vik? Would the pack turn on them? They were the only ones defending me, it seemed. I laid out my weapons and counted them, then packed them all up and started pacing. Vik and Thorsteinn risked everything for me. It was my fault it took so long to bond. Why was I so stupid?

A howl broke out in the distance. A lone wolf, its voice rising in pitch and volume until another overtook it. And another. And another—a whole host of wolves singing in eerie harmony. I rubbed my arms and paced some more.

Knut still hadn't moved from the foot of the tree. He didn't look up but kept his eyes on the path. A host of lights bobbed in the distance. A low murmur of voices, joining in with the wolves. The warriors were coming.

"Get her," they chanted. "Seize the murderer."

I stepped back from the lodge entrance and poured

water on the fire. My hands no longer shook. It was as if I expected it—the angry mob coming for me. They would overpower Knut and take me.

Tying my pack tight, I took the rolled-up ladder and snuck out a window on the opposite side of the lodge door. I shimmied out onto a branch. Vik and Thorsteinn had not taught me to climb, but I'd had plenty of practice hiding from nuns at the orphanage.

Head down, I crawled as far as the branch would allow.

The chorus of angry voices grew louder. At the foot of the tree, torches flared. A shout greeted them—Knut, commanding them to stop. He would not stop a mob.

Carefully, I tied the rope ladder to the branch and let it fall. A pause, while I waited for a shout to go up, a sign that they noticed me. All I heard was Knut speaking to the warriors, trying to reason with them. Then: a clang of metal on metal—weapons drawn.

I swung off the branch and scrambled down the ladder. I'd reached halfway when a shout went up.

"There—behind the tree! She's escaping!"

I leapt the rest of the way. The ground jarred my legs but after staggering sideways, I marshaled my balance enough to run.

From then on, it was a game. The warriors rushed after me; I ran into the undergrowth, dropping to my belly and crawling under briars while the warriors cursed and tried to come after me.

A wolf almost caught me when I exited, and I swung up into another tree, racing along, leaping from branch to branch.

I made the mistake of looking back, once. A fire grew in the sky. A sob caught in my throat when I realized what it was—Yggdrasil was burning. They'd set fire to my home.

Forcing my heavy legs onwards, I ducked and rolled down a steep hill, racing for the boundary of the mountain.

THORSTEINN

I STOOD with my arms crossed over my chest, facing the Alphas. Beside me, Vik fingered his axe.

"The raven is a messenger of Odin," one of the Alphas was telling the others. "We can hope the Corpse King does not use them for his evil purposes."

"Any word from the witches?"

"No. And Rosalind is awake but doesn't remember anything." The Alphas kept murmuring while we waited.

Finally, I cleared my throat.

"Patience, warrior," Samuel threw a sympathetic glance my way. "We are waiting for the pack to gather."

"With respect," I inclined my head. "We left our mate alone and promised to return to her shortly."

"So, you have mated her?" Daegan asked.

"The bond is new, but we believe it's strong," Vik reported. "But even if it would not survive a test, we claim Sorrel as mate. Anyone who wants her dead will feel the blade of my axe."

"Well said," Maddox thumped the arm of his seat. Ragnvald steepled his fingers, looking thoughtful. Samuel opened his mouth but before he could speak a shout made us turn.

"Thorsteinn! Vik!"

"Knut?" I bounded across the clearing to him. My weapon appeared in my hand.

"Fire in your lodge," he reported.

"Sorrel—?"

"Escaped."

"What? What is the meaning of this?" Samuel roared.

"A mob came for her," Knut said. "I could not stop them."

Samuel pounded the arm of his great throne, "I gave orders—"

"They disobeyed," Knut snapped.

"Sorrel," I whispered. As one, Vik and I clutched our weapons and ran from the clearing. We had to find our mate.

SORREL

I REACHED the boundary at the first light of dawn. There were no patrols of draugr in sight, but I hefted a rune stone anyway, glad I'd thought to pack some.

I hesitated at the foot of the hill, weighing my options. I could run and hide for a time, and hope Thorsteinn and Vik could find me. I couldn't leave tracks for them to find and risk the other warriors catching me.

Or, I could run without stopping, deep into enemy territory. I had the skills to survive. I could live in the wilderness for good. Just like I'd planned to, before the Berserkers captured me. I could be free.

But freedom wouldn't mean anything without Thorsteinn and Vik. I hadn't meant to let them in, but they knocked down my walls and stormed the door anyway.

Whipping out an arrow, I notched my bow and let it fly

striking a tree and pointing in the direction where I'd go. My warriors were expert trackers. They'd understand. They would find me.

I HAD ALMOST REACHED the border when a group of warriors stepped out from behind a cluster of birch.

"Got you," Ragnar said, and grabbed me by the jerkin.

I struggled, but they took my bow and arrow and knives, and pulled a bag over my head.

*V*IK

WE REACHED the lodge just as the final planks caught fire. Ash and burning wood rained down. A few warriors stood around and cheered. Thorsteinn shoved them aside, ignoring their shouted insults. We had to find Sorrel.

"This way," I ran to the remnants of the ladder. Someone had smeared pitch onto it so it'd burn. The charred ends smoked high above our heads. "She dropped to the ground here." I pointed to the set of footprints. "She ran that way, into the brambles."

"She's carrying a pack," Thorsteinn muttered.

"She knew the lodge would be attacked. She left before it happened," I said sharply. "She did not leave us." I brushed by him roughly, hoping it was true.

"We need to find her." We raced down the hill, leaving our burning home behind.

SORREL

MY WORLD WAS DARKNESS. The bag covered my face and body, the rough threads rubbing my face. The scent of dirt surrounded me. I swallowed my nausea as the warrior carried me like a sack of potatoes, uncaring how he jostled me. My heart beat in panic and I gritted my teeth so I wouldn't cry out. Thorsteinn and Vik would come for me. They would find me.

"Here we are," someone grunted, and my world turned upside down. I landed on the ground, stunned for a moment. Someone grabbed my leg and flipped me, and I was falling, falling.

I landed in darkness. Overhead a few warriors leaned over the pit where they'd thrown me.

"There. That'll teach her."

"No please," I lifted my hands to the sky, but the darkness covered the round hole and sealed away the sun.

Everything went dark.

THORSTEINN

"THERE." I pointed to the path of disturbed leaves marking Sorrel's path. "She went towards the boundary."

"Of course she did," Vik said. "She knows how to survive out there. We taught her."

He took off and I ran beside him. "We must consider that she does not want to be found. She took her pack. Stores for food—"

"No," Vik said. "She did not run from us."

"She may have. Women always leave."

"She is not any woman. She is ours," he bellowed. His skin cracked and fur sprouted down his arm. Soon the beast would break free.

That's when I saw the arrow, the fletch fluttering high above our heads. "Look there," I shouted, and Vik grunted. We turned and raced the way the arrow pointed.

"Forgive me, Sorrel," I muttered to myself as I ran. "I never should've doubted you."

～

SORREL

A MOANING SOUND filled the pit. My hand flew to my throat and I realized the sound came from me. It cut off abruptly and there was nothing. No noise. No light. My heart beat pounded in my ears.

Something rustled in the dark. Blackness rose up to swallow me. Soon there would be no Sorrel. There would be nothing of me left.

"Let me out," It came out a croak but inside my head, I was screaming.

The darkness would eat me alive. But when I closed my eyes there was a flash of light.

There! A light around the door. Just a crack, just enough. *Thorsteinn? Vik? Help me!*

～

VIK

.   .   .

WE RAN AS MONSTERS, tracking Sorrel. Her trail led to the boundary... straight into a waiting group of warriors. We followed their tracks and lost them in a mountain stream.

"Where is she?" Thorsteinn raged.

I cursed. The forest spun in a circle.

Leaves flew as Thorsteinn fell to all fours and raked the earth with his claws.

Vik, Sorrel's voice whispered.

"Sorrel?" I whirled. "Where?"

The beast that was Thorsteinn swiveled his great black head towards me.

Do you hear that? I asked via our mind link.

The beast grunted.

Vik. Thorsteinn. Help!

Sorrel, we both stretched our minds towards hers. *Speak to us.*

Help me!

We both were running, the forest a blur around us.

What happened? Where are you?

I... I left the lodge. I had to. She sniffled. She was somewhere crouched in the dark. Alone, afraid. She hated the dark.

We know. Thorsteinn answered, sounding reasonably like himself, for all he was a fur covered monster racing beside me, sometimes on two feet, sometimes on four.

I ran to the boundary. The warriors caught me, and I can't get out.

Stay with us, Sorrel, I said. *Keep talking. We're coming. Do you know where they took you?*

Silence.

Then: a mindless wail.

The dark the dark the dark

"Darkness." I mused aloud. "She hates the dark. But only when it closes around her, like in a pit..." I stopped as Thorsteinn roared beside me.

"I know where she is," I told him, and headed back to the place of the standing stones.

SORREL

DARKNESS CLAWED AT ME, crawling down my throat. I couldn't speak. I could only reach out in my mind.

Vik. Thorsteinn. Please...

Sorrel? Sorrel!

I'm here. They caught me—I shared the image.

Stay calm, little warrior, we are coming.

A roar reached my ears. Someone was scrabbling at the stone covering my prison. I shrank back into darkness in case my captors had returned to torment me.

A body plummeted to the bottom to the pit.

Sorrel, the beast growled. Vik, his body huge and shaped like a monster, grey fur sprouting from his massive arms and torso. His face was elongated into a wolf's muzzle, his fangs long and gleaming but I felt no fear. I ran to him.

Vik!

Sorrel. It's me. I am here.

He hefted me against his hard torso, helping me shift to his back. *Hold tight,* he ordered.

I clung to him as he dug his wicked claws into the sides of the pit. His feet were giant paws. He dug them into the wall and began to climb.

VIK

I PULLED us from the pit just in time to meet a mob. Thorsteinn danced with a trio of warriors, spinning, thrusting, parrying their blows with his axe.

I herded Sorrel behind me, roaring as I faced another group of warriors.

"Cowards," I raged. "Attacking our defenseless mate."

"She tried to murder a spaewife," a warrior's shout ended in a gargle. He ripped an arrow from his throat, his face contorting as the beast took over his form.

Sorrel straightened behind me, her face bloodless. She nodded to me and notched another arrow in her bow.

"You shouldn't have left my weapons so close to the pit," she snarled, and loosed another arrow into the fray.

Laughing wildly, I waded into the fight, swinging my axe.

SORREL

ALL AROUND, warriors raged, cursing me and calling for my blood.

Thorsteinn and Vik held the line, hulking monsters covered in silver or black fur. They kept the mob from reaching me, but I was not helpless. I backed up to a rocky outcropping and chose my targets carefully, shooting over the monsters' heads.

"Enough," a blond warrior roared. I angled my bow

upwards as he and the three Alphas joined the fight. Two dark-haired Alphas, one covered in tattoos, attacked viciously, pulling Berserkers off Thorsteinn and Vik and growling for the opposing mob to back down.

A flutter of black feathers caught my eyes. There, circling over the fight, was a raven. In its claws glinted a familiar stone.

"The moonstone," I gasped. I was out of arrows. Reaching in my pockets, I drew out the rune stones, picked a patch of bare ground, and threw them down.

The blast shook the clearing. Berserkers fell to their knees, coughing in the acrid smoke.

My head was ringing when Thorsteinn and Vik crawled to me.

"Sorrel? Are you hurt?"

"No," I coughed. "But there was a raven—look—"

A flash and a woman appeared between us and the Alphas. Her hair was a silver-gold braid crowning her head. She wore a simple shift that left her arms and legs bare.

"Enough," she ordered, her low voice somehow ringing over the warriors. The shouting ceased.

"Yseult," The Alpha Samuel greeted her, wiping grit from his red eyes.

Four huge warriors, clad in armor like I'd never seen, clanked forward and surrounded the blonde witch, blocking anyone's view of her. Just as well, something in her face was too terrible to look at directly.

"I see I have come just in time," she said, crossing her arms over her chest.

"Get these warriors out of here," Samuel ordered, and the Alphas began shoving the unruly pack members out of the clearing. "Obey or we'll throw you in the pit," one Alpha muttered.

"Who threw balefire?" Samuel asked.

"I did," I spoke up. "I saw a raven with the moonstone and didn't know what else to do."

"You did well," Vik whispered to me. He and Thorsteinn stood squarely in front of me, protecting me just like the four armored guards protected the witch.

"I have the moonstone," she said, holding it aloft. It glinted in the morning light, washing us in a soft glow. "One of my sisters was flying over the land and saw it. She brought it to me. I did not know of the events with these spaewives until you sent word."

"Can she bear witness to what happened?"

The witch nodded. "Her view was warped because she was in raven form, but now she can speak of it. She saw a spaewife entranced by the Corpse King, and another rise up and strike her down."

I winced but the witch went on. "Without Sorrel, the moonstone would have been lost. Because of her we have what we need. With the moonstone we will defeat the Corpse King."

8

S orrel

THE ALPHAS BID us wait in the cave while they conferred further with the witch. Vik and Thorsteinn refused to leave my side, even when one suggested they should not leave me with two Berserkers in monster form.

"Sorrel does not fear them. Why should we interfere?" The quiet blond Alpha, Ragnvald, winked at me.

Inside the cave, I submitted to the warriors pawing over me, checking for wounds. "I'm fine. You came for me before I was harmed."

"We never should've left. We will not do so again."

I swallowed around a lump in my throat. "The mob burned our home."

"We will build another." Vik caught my hand. "Sorrel, you reached out to us."

"I had to, did I not?" I flushed. "It was the only way. I did not want you to think I left you."

"I doubted for a moment," Thorsteinn admitted. "But then I saw the arrow and knew you ran from the mob, and not from us."

I pulled him down by his braid and kissed him madly. Vik tugged me to him and took his turn. We were all breathing heavily when I broke away.

"What of the mob? Will the pack ever accept me?"

Vik started to answer when a shadow fell across the door.

Ragnvald beckoned. "The Alphas will see you now."

The corridor to the Alpha's chamber seemed shorter this time. Or perhaps the torches burned brighter. The room Ragnvald led us into held four wooden thrones, but none of the Alphas sat. I hesitated on the threshold and gripped my mate's hands tighter.

"Come, Sorrel," Samuel beckoned me. He wasn't exactly smiling, but his brow was smooth, his countenance lighter. To my shock he went on bended knee to speak to me. His leonine head was level with mine. "How are you feeling?"

"I am well, sir," I answered at Thorsteinn's nudge. If the warriors were worried I'd cause a scene here, they needn't be. All the fight had left me after I threw the rune stones.

"There is much to say, and even more to be done. You'll forgive us if we keep things short. Sorrel, you're absolved of all wrongdoing. You're free to go."

"What about Rosalind?" I asked. "Will she be in trouble."

"Rosalind is still recovering. Maybe, if she remembers her actions, she will have a chance to atone."

"It wasn't her fault," I said. "The Corpse King tricked her,

I know it. He—" I fell silent as Vik pulled me back against him.

"We know, Sorrel," Samuel murmured. "We will not judge her too harshly."

"And the moonstone?" Thorsteinn asked.

"Safe with the witches. They are gathering here now. If all goes well, we will soon march to overthrow our enemy."

"The warriors who attacked Sorrel—they will go unpunished?" Vik asked.

"We will send them to be first in the line of attack," Samuel said.

"Their punishment is light because we need them," Ragnvald added.

Thorsteinn growled.

"It's all right," I squeezed my warrior's hands. "The Corpse King has stirred up enough trouble. Let us not war amongst ourselves."

"Well said," muttered the tattooed Alpha.

"It will not be wise to let Sorrel free on the mountain until the march has begun," Samuel said. "We can offer you safe haven in here. My mate will prepare quarters—"

"No," Thorsteinn turned me to him and cupped my face. "Do you trust us?"

I nodded. *Always.*

"What do you mean, Thorsteinn?" Ragnvald asked.

"Alphas, I have a solution." Thorsteinn settled his hands on my shoulders. "If the pack will not accept Sorrel, we will leave."

"But," Samuel said, "We need you—"

"Send us away. All three. We will patrol the farthest reaches and will not return until the Corpse King is defeated."

Silence fell. The Alpha's expressions ranged from thoughtfulness to disbelief.

"You would put your mate at risk?" The tattooed Alpha asked, almost angry.

"She is well trained," Vik said.

"She will not be at risk. She will be with us."

"She is definitely a fighter," Samuel mused. Vik snickered.

Ragnvald cleared his throat. "Sorrel, does this satisfy you? Will you go with them?"

"Yes. They need me to defend them," I said.

Vik laughed again, two of the Alphas with him.

A smile cracked the head Alpha's face. "Very well," Samuel waved his hand. "Call us if you need aid. I will wait on your report."

"Come," Vik whispered, herding me towards the door.

"Keep your mate safe," Ragnvald called after us. "We will need her to fight with us when we face the enemy."

SORREL

WE STOOD ON THE BOUNDARY, facing the enemies' ranks. Rows and rows of draugr, pressing their slavering faces against the magical boundary.

Vik pressed a rune stone in my hand. The rest went into a pouch, ready for me to reload. He and Thorsteinn took their places beside me, axes and shields at the ready, their own packs strapped to their back. The Alphas had loaded us up with supplies to last us until we reached the first patrol station where Thorsteinn and Vik kept stores. The way would be hard and long, but with my mates at my side I would be safe. "An adventure," Vik called it. "A life in the wilderness, just as you wanted." Thorsteinn had ruffled my hair.

"Ready?" Thorsteinn asked. He and Vik flanked me.

"Ready," I shouted, and ran with my warriors into the wild.

EPILOGUE

R osalind

"ROSALIND." A cool breeze wafted over my face. I opened my eyes, squinting against the pounding in my head.

"I'm awake," I croaked. My visitor was a tall blonde woman wearing a white shift that left her arms bare. Her features were too strong to be counted beautiful, but once I met her eyes, I couldn't look away. "Why are you here?"

The past few days had been filled with visitors. My sister Aspen was the only one I'd welcomed. The rest seemed determined to ask me questions. I'd answered best I could despite the blinding pain, but I wasn't much help. Other than a few shadowy nightmares, my memory was gone.

"Can you sit up?" the woman asked. "Do you wish for water?"

I opened my mouth to tell her to leave me alone, when

she waved a hand over my forehead. Instantly, the pain eased.

"Do that again," I gasped.

A smile lightened the woman's features. "Most wouldn't survive such an injury. You have a hard head. Or a strong will to live."

My life was one determined fight to survive. I didn't remember much, but I knew that.

"I am Yseult," said the woman, seating herself on the side of my pallet. "I am a witch."

"What do you want?"

In answer, she fished in the front of her shift, and drew out a shimmering stone on a silver chain.

My eyes widened as bright light bathed my face. "Get that away from me."

"You remember this?" Yseult cupped her hand around the large stone, hiding some of its brilliance. "You seem to have forgotten everything else."

"I remember the stone. I had to find it. I don't know why."

"The Alphas think you were bespelled by the Corpse King and tricked into finding it for him."

I lay back on my pallet. "I know. I'd be named a traitor, if I were well."

"They will not judge a spaewife so harshly," Ysuelt waved her free hand. The stone in her other hand flashed and I looked away, my stomach lurching. "I am more interested in how you knew where to find the stone."

"Couldn't the Corpse King lead me to it?"

"Perhaps. But the stone has its own protections. Which is why the enemy needed you to fetch it for him." She opened her hand and frowned at the stone, her face bathed in milky light.

I shut my eyes before my headache returned.

"I had dreams," I admitted. "Visions. I knew where the stone would be. But the voice calling me from the mountain —that was all the Corpse King."

"Not only him. If you had been fully under his influence, you would never had found the stone." Yseult shifted closer. "No, Rosalind. The affinity you have for this talisman is the key we have been searching for."

I ran a hand over my face. I was so tired. "What do you mean?"

"I too have had visions. My witch sisters and I have Seen the way to defeat the Corpse King, but in every vision, you are there."

Somehow, I wasn't surprised. I felt like I was viewing this conversation from afar, a bird circling overhead, a seer looking into a scrying pool at myself. Another vision. I was so tired of visions.

I licked my lips. "It doesn't matter what you saw. I am here. I am hurt."

"The Alphas will pass judgement on you soon. They will give you to a pair of warriors as a mate."

I raised a hand and slapped it down. "They'll do what they will. That's why they brought us here—to be mates."

"You do not want to be mated?"

"No. I will never..." I fisted my hands in the pelts. "I will never belong to any man. Ever. This I vow."

"You want to have a choice."

"Yes," I fell back against my bed. "But I have no power."

Yseult leaned closer. "You do not think you can decide your own destiny?"

My body stiffened. "All my life I have been a pawn. Even when I fought for freedom, I was being manipulated by the

Corpse King. He promised me protection," my voice cracked as I confessed what I'd told no one. "For me and my sister. We would be safe. We would escape the Berserkers, and live free."

"What if it were possible? You could bind the Corpse King and end his reign? The Berserkers would give you anything you ask for then. Even your freedom."

"It is not possible. Even if I wanted to, how can I face the Corpse King? The greatest enemy the world has ever known?"

"There is a way, Rosalind. I fear it is the only way."

I squeezed my eyes shut. The ache in my head was gone as if it'd never been. In its place was a hollow fear. If the Corpse King took over, my sister's and my life would be over. If I stayed here, we would be given to Berserkers as brides. There was no good choice for us. For women, there rarely was.

"What would I need to do?"

"My sister witches and I have a plan..."

SORREL

"COME ON," Vik shouted. I raced up the hill behind him, heart pounding, legs aching. Behind us, Thorsteinn paused long enough to throw a rune stone at the draugr chasing us. The blast made me stagger. A cloud of dirt and smoke enveloped me. Thorsteinn hauled me up and propelled me up the ridge. I rubbed my eyes, coughing a little.

"Thanks," I croaked.

"You're all right," he tousled my hair, and guarded my back as I took off after Vik.

"We're close," Vik said. "Just over the ridge."

"Hurry," I said. My throat screamed for water and fresh air, but I couldn't help my grin. We'd spent days trekking the wilderness towards the Corpse King's lair, dodging hosts of draugr, sleeping under the stars. Vik and Thorsteinn told me of their patrol station, a hidden place protected with ward runes right in the heart of enemy territory. We were almost there when we ran into the final contingent of draugr.

"How many rune stones do we have left?" Thorsteinn asked as we rested behind a crop of boulders.

"Just one," I answered grimly.

"We'll get more soon. For now, one's enough." He showed me his three and jerked a thumb behind him, a signal of where to throw. A grunting sound behind us told me the draugr were right on our heels.

"On my count," he ordered. "One, two, three—"

Rising up together, we threw the stones into the grotesque ranks of the enemy's servants. Balefire flashed. I ducked back behind the rock, only to be pulled along by Vik.

"Run," he said, and we made our final dash.

"Vik," I panted, my legs pumping to keep up. We were running straight for a huge tree. "What—"

"Up," he said, and raced the final steps ahead of me to the massive trunk. "Now." He dropped to his knees and laced his fingers. I sprinted and leapt, my foot landing in his cupped hands. He launched me in the air, and I grabbed the branch, swinging up as quickly as possible.

"Climb," he called and, checking his weapons, started to do the same. I launched myself from branch to branch, sparing glances to make sure Thorsteinn was coming too. Above my head, a floor board peeked out from the foliage.

"A tree lodge," I whispered.

"Yes," Vik grunted, grinning.

"Where's Thorsteinn?"

A roar shook the forest. Thorsteinn tore out of the trees, a flash of black fur with teeth. Monstrous claws sank into the tree bark as he climbed.

Vik was suddenly above me, pulling me onto a wooden platform. A few boards were hammered into the tree trunk, leading to a final large enclosure nestled in the huge canopy. My feet thumped the sturdy wooden floor as Vik went straight to a hidden store and struck a flintstone to light a small brazier.

"This is it?" I asked, turning in a circle. "It's just like Yggdrasil."

"This is one of many Yggdrasils," Vik told me, grinning at my delight. He went around the perimeter, lighting the rest of the braziers. The place was well stocked with water-skins, weapons, and baskets with stored food. "We build these as hiding places when we are on long patrols. Here," he tossed me his waterskin. "Drink up. There's a stream nearby. This tree and the waters close to it are protected by wards the witches gave us."

Water splashed down my throat, washing the last of the smoke and grit away. "Thank you," I held the skin out to him. He grabbed it, finished the water, and tossed it aside.

"Sorrel," his teeth flashed and I recognized the wicked light in his eye a moment before he pounced. His hand fisted in my hair, his mouth meeting mine hungrily.

"Vik—" I laughed against his lips. With a growl, he tugged my hair and continued his savage kiss. His cock poked my belly as he propelled me backwards. Before I could ask where we were going, he hooked my foot out from under me. We fell onto a pile of pelts.

"Vik," I tried again as he pinned my arms above my head, his beard scratching down my throat as he ravaged me. "What are you doing?"

"What do you think I'm doing?" His left hand kept hold of my wrists, freeing his right hand to grip my breast.

"No?"

"I am tired and so dirty—"

"Not so dirty," he hitched my leg over his back and ground down. "Are you so very tired?"

"Not too tired—" I whispered, pulling his full weight against me. A growl behind us told me Thorsteinn had arrived. Vik and I paused as he shrank from his monstrous form into a warrior's. He stalked towards us, eyes bright.

"Getting started without me?" he rasped.

Vik sat back and let me up. Thorsteinn plucked me off the pelts and hauled me against him. My legs hooked around his hips as he claimed my mouth. When he broke the kiss, his voice was more normal.

"You did well, little shield maiden." He pressed his forehead against mine.

"Do you think so?" I whispered back, joy shooting through my body.

"Oh yes." He set me down and two pairs of hands pawed at my body, quickly divesting me of my clothes. "And now we celebrate."

"I'd like that," I gasped as Vik dropped to his knees before me. He propped my leg over his shoulder and nuzzled between my thighs. Thorsteinn clamped an arm around my waist, his mouth biting and sucking the tender junction of my neck.

"Here," he said, probing a finger between my ass cheeks.

"What? No—" I yelped as Vik bit the inside of my leg.

"Be good, or we'll build another cage..." His wicked grin sent a surge of arousal through me.

"I'll cage you," I threatened, and fought the men holding me. We wrestled together, playful and savage, until they ended it, pinning me down. Thorsteinn fed me his cock while Vik plundered between my legs.

"HOW DID YOU KNOW," I murmured later, much later, after they had washed me and fed me bits of meat and held me down and taken me again.

"What, sweet one?" Thorsteinn murmured, toying with the ends of my hair.

I yawned. "How did you know I could go on patrol with you?"

"You were born for this. We knew it from the first, when you shot at us in the abbey. You come alive when you are in danger. We will just be careful to keep you safe..."

I made a face at him and he kissed it away.

"I thought you would be worried," I admitted when I could speak again. "The mist warped my mind before."

"We're bonded now. The bond will protect you, just as it calms the beast. You have nothing to fear. No harm will come to you... unless we decide to hurt you." He set his teeth gently at my neck.

"And even then, you will like it," Vik promised, coming to lie beside me opposite his warrior brother. "You were born to wear our mark. Just as we were born to love you..."

My heart swelled with happiness, I climbed on top of

him to give him a reward. Outside the mist swirled around the base of the tree and the draugr roamed, guarding the Corpse King's territory. In the morning, we would face the enemy and gather any knowledge we could to aid the pack. It would be dangerous, but I did not fear. I did not fear anything—as long as I had my warriors.

THANK YOU FOR READING! Mastered by the Berserkers is next.

FREE BOOK

Get two secret Berserker books, Bred by the Berserkers and
A Berserker Birth, available exclusively to you:

https://geni.us/BredBerserkerNONL
https://geni.us/BirthBerserkerNONL

A NOTE FROM LEE SAVINO

Hey there. It's me, Lee Savino. I'm so glad you read this book and ordered it directly from my store. Readers like you make my author life possible! And being an author is a dream come true.

If you're like me, you're wondering what to read next. Let me help you out...

If you haven't yet, check out the two exclusive extras I wrote in the Berserker world. They're available here:

Bred by the Berserkers
https://geni.us/BredBerserkerNONL

A Berserker Birth
https://geni.us/BirthBerserkerNONL

And if you want more Berserkers, you can find the complete selection at my store or get the 15 book bundle here!

WANT MORE BERSERKERS?

These fierce warriors will stop at nothing to claim their mates...

Get a 15 e-book Berserker bundle on sale at my Lee Savino shop!

The Berserker Saga

Sold to the Berserkers – Brenna, Samuel & Daegan
Mated to the Berserkers – Brenna, Samuel & Daegan
Bred by the Berserkers (FREE novella only available to you)
– Brenna, Samuel & Daegan
Taken by the Berserkers – Sabine, Ragnvald & Maddox
Given to the Berserkers – Muriel and her mates
Claimed by the Berserkers – Fleur and her mates
Rescued by the Berserker – Hazel & Knut
Captured by the Berserkers – Willow, Leif & Brokk
Kidnapped by the Berserkers – Sage, Thorbjorn & Rolf
Bonded to the Berserkers – Laurel, Haakon & Ulf

Berserker Babies – the sisters Brenna, Sabine, Muriel, Fleur
and their mates
Night of the Berserkers – the witch Yseult's story
Owned by the Berserkers – Fern, Dagg & Svein
Tamed by the Berserkers – Sorrel, Thorsteinn & Vik
Mastered by the Berserkers – Juliet, Jarl & Fenrir
Surrendered to the Berserkers – Rosalind and her mates

Berserker Warriors

Ægir *(formerly titled The Sea Wolf)*
Siebold with Ines Johnson

ALSO BY LEE SAVINO

For film and TV rights inquiries: <u>lee.savino@leesavino.com</u>

Paranormal romance

Berserker Saga

Sold to the Berserkers

Mated to the Berserkers

Bred by the Berserkers (FREE novella only available at www.leesavino.com)

Taken by the Berserkers

Given to the Berserkers

Claimed by the Berserkers

Rescued by the Berserker

Captured by the Berserkers

Kidnapped by the Berserkers

Bonded to the Berserkers

Berserker Babies

Night of the Berserkers

Owned by the Berserkers

Tamed by the Berserkers

Mastered by the Berserkers

Surrendered to the Berserkers

Berserker Warriors

Aegir

Siebold with Ines Johnson

Bad Boy Alphas with Renee Rose

Alpha's Temptation

Alpha's Danger

Alpha's Prize

Alpha's Challenge

Alpha's Obsession

Alpha's Desire

Alpha's War

Alpha's Mission

Alpha's Bane

Alpha's Secret

Alpha's Prey

Alpha's Sun

Shifter Ops with Renee Rose

Alpha's Moon

Alpha's Vow

Alpha's Revenge

Alpha's Fire

Alpha's Rescue

Alpha's Command

Midnight Doms with Renee Rose

Alpha's Blood

His Captive Mortal

The Virgin and the Vampire

(All Souls' Night anthology exclusive)

Werewolves of Wallstreet with Renee Rose

Big Bad Boss: Midnight

Big Bad Boss: Moon Mad

Big Bad Boss: Marked

Sci fi romance

Planet of Kings with Tabitha Black

Brutal Mate

Brutal Claim

Brutal Capture

Brutal Beast

Brutal Demon

Tsenturion Warriors with Golden Angel

Alien Captive

Alien Tribute

Alien Abduction

Dragons in Exile with Lili Zander

Draekon Mate

Draekon Fire

Draekon Heart

Draekon Abduction

Draekon Destiny

Daughter of Draekons

Draekon Fever

Draekon Rogue

Draekon Holiday

Draekon Rebel Force with Lili Zander

Draekon Warrior

Draekon Conqueror

Draekon Pirate

Draekon Warlord

Draekon Guardian

Contemporary Romance

Royally Bad

Royally Fake Fiancé

Her Marine Daddy

Her Dueling Daddies

Beauty & The Lumberjacks

Snowed in with the Lumberjack

Rescuing Regina

Dark Mafia Romance

Mafia Brides

Revenge is Sweet

Vengeance is Mine

A Dark Mafia Romance trilogy with Stasia Black

Innocence

Awakening

Queen of the Underworld

Beauty and the Rose trilogy with Stasia Black

Beauty's Beast

Beauty & the Thorns

Beauty & the Rose

Cowboy Romance

Rocky Mountain Mail Order Brides

Rocky Mountain Dawn

Rocky Mountain Bride

Rocky Mountain Rose

Rocky Mountain Romp

Rocky Mountain Rogue

Rocky Mountain Daddy

Rocky Mountain Ride

Possessing Pearl

Wild Whip Ranch with Tristan River

Cowboy's Babygirl

Taming His Wild Girl

ABOUT THE AUTHOR

USA today bestselling author Lee Savino has written over 69 steamy romance novels. Bad boys, mafia men, wolf shifters, and dragon shifters in space—her dominant, alpha-hole heroes will stop at nothing to possess their one true love. Happily-ever-after and book hangover guaranteed!

Connect with Lee Savino in her fabulous Goddess Group:
https://www.facebook.com/groups/LeeSavino